TIN

CANDACE ROBINSON & AMBER R. DUELL

Midnight Tide
PUBLISHING

FOR ELLE

CHAPTER ONE

TIN

❖———————❖

Tin picked absently at the dried blood on his iron-tipped gloves. Day had turned to night with no sign of his target. Lord save the ugly bastard if he was off killing the brownie who'd hired him. She still owed Tin half his money, payable only when the dwarf's head was delivered. The dwarf was as good as dead either way, if only because Tin was stuck perched in the damn tree for so long, but he was a professional.

And professionals got paid.

With an exaggerated huff, Tin pried his iron axe from where it was imbedded in the tree near his head. An unusual weapon for a faerie, but he had long ago embraced the pain of iron. He had no choice, really—it was that or go mad. Almost as mad as this dwarf was making him. It was no wonder someone wanted the miner dead.

A light-skinned sprite landed on the branch just above him, all spindly limbs and unkempt hair. She seemed oblivious to Tin's presence as she plucked delicate white leaves from the otherwise-green foliage and tucked them into a little basket on her arm. Her wings shook, golden pollen raining down.

Tin jerked away from the shimmering powder before it landed in his long silver hair, and snatched the sprite in a blindingly fast motion. The tiny creature shrieked inside his closed fist, then fell silent as he tightened his grip until bones crunched.

"Nasty creature," he spat, though sprites weren't particularly bothersome, and unfurled his fingers. Bits of sprite coated his gloved hand. He brushed it off the best he could, wiping the remnants on his pants.

The sprite's innards weren't the only relic of a kill to adorn his clothing. Kelpie scales were artfully sewn into his dark clothing for extra protection, and the small rings holding the right side of his hair back were whittled from their blackened bones.

A low whistle sounded in the distance, the tune cheerful and carefree. Tin gripped his axe tighter and leapt lithely from the tree, landing silently in the grass. He edged around the wide trunk and peered in the direction of the lighthearted song.

The dwarf he'd been waiting for crested the hill with a massive pack strapped to his back. Over his shoulder, a pickaxe was visible in the moonlight, the handle tucked safely away. His hands were empty. Good. It was annoying when they fought back.

Tin held his breath and watched his mark close the distance between them. The dwarf had a gnarled beard, ratty, knotted black hair, and a bulbous nose, all of which were coated in dark powder from the mineral mines. Suddenly, Tin regretted not bringing a bag to carry the head in. Mineral powder was even harder to wash from around the kelpie scales than pixie dust. Alas…

The dwarf was still whistling his merry tune when Tin leapt from his hiding place, axe swinging. His mark flailed and his heavy pack pulled him backward where he landed in a heap. "Wait! I—"

2

His eyes went wide and he sucked in a breath as the moonlight flashed over Tin's face. The mark of shame—or as Tin thought of it, his badge of honor—was known in every corner of Oz. The Wizard had taken *pity* on him after Tin's heart turned back into stone. Instead of being sentenced to death for assassinating eleven fae lords, he'd been branded. Shackled and bound, he'd been unable to escape as liquid iron was dripped slowly onto the side of his face. Each drop had landed at the edge of his cheekbone where it scalded a path across his skin. By the time it was finished and the iron cooled, Tin had been left with a design of wild, twisting silver lines that covered nearly half his right cheek.

"Have mercy," the dwarf begged.

Tin grinned savagely. The Wizard should've killed him. "There is no mercy in this world."

"Why?" the dwarf asked in a cracking voice. "I've done nothing!"

"Everyone has done *something*."

Tin swung his axe, severing the target's head before he could scream. He bent, fisting the dingy hair. Bright red blood gushed from the neck as he lifted the proof of his work. As he sauntered back toward the brownie's house to collect the rest of his fee, leaving a red trail in his wake, he whistled the end of the dwarf's song.

Firelight and music reached the brownie's cave from the nearby village. When Tin arrived, he found the old female atop a rock outside the opening, swaying to the song as she waited for him. Thin wisps of white hair floated around her molting head. Toenails curled over the ends of her feet. Age spots marked her olive skin, just as red stripes decorated her loose dress.

"You're late," she snapped.

"What do you care? He's dead." Tin threw the bloody head

3

at the brownie, nearly knocking the portly faerie off the rock. This job was too far below his skill-set—and his pay grade—for him to put up with snide comments.

"I hired you to kill him *before* sundown."

Tin cracked his neck. It would be more profitable to kill the brownie and take whatever valuables she owned. She was ancient and barely came to his knee—it would be easy—but if he began killing his clientele, no one would seek him out. It was already hard enough finding work outside of the Emerald City. Country folk weren't much in the way of intrigue like those in the capital, but they made up for it with their ruthlessness. If the fae here didn't take care of their own problems, no one would.

The brownie must've sensed the shift in Tin's thoughts because she made a show of checking the validity of the head. "Fine. It's done." She reached down the front of her dress for a small bag. She pretended to weigh it in her hands before tossing it at his feet. "This concludes our business, assassin."

He caught the bag with the toe of his boot just before it landed in the dirt. It took every ounce of his meager self-control not to lunge for her throat. Tin opened the bag to be sure it was full of diamonds and not pebbles, though he was confident the brownie wasn't stupid enough to swindle him. The last person who'd tried that ended up impaled.

Satisfied, he turned on his heel and walked toward the town for a well-deserved drink. If he could find a room for the night, and someone to buy the gemstones off him before he moved to the next town, all the better.

Glimpses of fae flashed through the trees as he neared the edge of the clearing. Vivid, gem-colored fabric swirled around their lithe bodies. The firelight caressed exposed skin, some pale, some dark, some flecked with scales and others with feathers. Ribbons tied to posts lifted and fell in time with their flawless movements.

It seemed a nightly ritual in this part of Oz to greet the dawn with dance, which meant they would be at it all night. He'd never stepped foot in this particular town and wasn't sure what their reaction to him might be. Sometimes they called for his head, other times they hid inside and bolted the doors. Often it was a mixture of both. Whatever the response to his iron scars, Tin didn't much care unless it created extra work for himself.

Tin touched the rings in his hair without meaning to. He refused to hide his face, even if it made things easier, so he dropped his hand and strode straight into the town and through the party. The dancers faltered as they noticed him. Hooves ceased stomping, wings stilled, and soon the music sputtered out as well.

Tin made an exaggerated bow and held his breath. When no one screamed or made to attack, Tin dodged the decorative floating balls of light on his way to the tavern. It was better to hurry before they made up their minds on how to respond. The sign for the Peppered Pike hung crooked over the door in elvish writing. He steeled himself for the owner to give him the boot the moment he stepped inside, but he could really do with a night in an actual bed. Right after a drink.

Inside, the tavern was empty save for a female wiping down the bar. Two ribbed horns circled the sides of her head and her dark hair was styled to run parallel with them. "Welco—" Her words cut off as her gaze met his, recognizing him immediately.

Tin did his best to give her a reassuring smile but the iron distorted half of it. "Do you have any rooms?"

The girl shifted back warily. "We're … closed … during the…"

He didn't mention that she'd started to welcome him before she looked up. Instead, he pulled out one of the larger diamonds and held it in the center of his palm. Her eyes grew impossibly wide at the sight of all the fresh blood on his glove.

Shit. Diamond or no diamond, he knew she was five seconds away from bolting.

"Give the man a room, sweetmeat."

Tin froze at the familiar voice—one he blissfully hadn't

heard in years—and eyed the alcohol behind the bar. "What are you doing here, Lion?"

"Good. You remember who I am," he said with a chuckle. "Join me."

The last time Tin saw the bastard was at his hearing, when Lion was called as a witness against him. For all the courage Lion gained, it had only made him a fool. Tin ground his teeth together and turned to face the other fae. Lion was exactly as he remembered: coarse golden hair tied in a low ponytail, bronze skin, and piercing golden eyes. The tuft at the end of his tawny tail skimmed the floor beside his boots. A fur cloak wrapping around Lion's broad shoulders made him appear even larger.

But, no matter how much bigger Lion was, Tin was certain he wasn't a threat. Lion had a heart, after all, even if it was darker than most, and that bloody organ made all creatures weak.

"What are you doing out of the South?" Tin growled.

Lion smirked arrogantly and flicked a look at the tavern girl, who let out a sharp gasp from behind the bar. "Another drink, if you wouldn't mind, and one for my friend."

"I asked you a question."

Lion rolled his eyes. "Stop being an ass and sit down."

Tin drew a slow, steady breath and reached for the axe at his hip.

"You're going to scare the lady," Lion warned coolly.

The hell if he cared. "I warned you. If I ever saw you again—"

"We're immortal, Tin. There's plenty of time to kill me. I have a job for you, so you may as well make your fortune first."

Fortune. Tin kept his hand on his axe but didn't wield it. He didn't kill people because he needed money—he *liked* killing— but that wasn't to say that he didn't recognize its usefulness.

The horned female sat the drinks down on the table with shaking hands. Some of the foam splashed over the sides, landing on Lion's sleeve. He growled at her and she hurtled out the back door.

Once they were alone, Lion continued. "You remember Dorothy, don't you?"

Tin narrowed his eyes, his grip tightening on his weapon. It was rather hard to forget the little human girl who'd crashed into his life and set him on the path to self-destruction.

"Of course you remember the little bitch." Lion took a long gulp of his drink, studying Tin over the rim of the glass. He nudged the empty chair across from him with his boot. Another invitation to sit.

This time, Tin accepted.

Chapter Two

Dorothy

Dorothy gripped the handle of the garden fork so hard that her palm would most likely bleed. With the tool and gritted teeth, she ripped a carrot from the dirt—then another and another and another. Her fierce actions were scarring the flesh of the vegetables, but she didn't care because she needed as many as possible.

Blowing out an exhausted breath, she stared at her aching hands—red and rubbed raw. She didn't mind the aches and pains. This farm had to survive, not only for her, but for Aunt Em and Uncle Henry. It had to.

Tears ran down her filthy cheeks, landing against her striped overalls as she thought about her aunt and uncle. Uncle Henry had been gone for five years now, and Aunt Em nine months. After Uncle Henry died from scarlet fever, most of the workers had left, and the farm's profits took a nose dive. The remaining workers had stopped showing up when Aunt Em passed from a heart attack. There was no way to make the business thrive with only Dorothy. Nobody in town wanted to work for Crazy

Dorothy Gale. No one.

She fisted a carrot, fingernails digging into the vegetable as she thought of the place that everyone had told her didn't exist—no matter how many times she screamed and yelled that it did. At times, she wasn't so sure what to believe anymore. A flash of emerald crawled into her thoughts and she closed her eyes, shutting out what Aunt Em had beaten into her head—it wasn't true.

"There's no place like home," she said through clenched teeth. "There's no place like home, Dorothy. Because this is the only place that's real. Oz never existed." She breathed heavily, remembering the needles, the pokes, the prods, the medicines, the shock therapy—all of it.

And still, the place lingered in her mind when she opened her eyes.

As Dorothy leaned back down to grab her shovel and return to the task she'd set for herself, a line of dust, farther out from the farm along the dirt road, filled the air with brown smoky clouds. She froze.

Dorothy recognized the black two-seater Roadster, and knew right away it was Jimmy. Time wasn't on her side anymore. Jimmy was a friend she'd known for years, but more importantly, he was the messenger for his father. His father, Glenn, had been trying to take the farm from under her feet for months. Dorothy had made the decision two weeks ago that the last way to possibly prevent the farm from being taken was to sleep with Jimmy. She liked him well enough, and she was desperate, but it was a terrible action on her part. A terrible action she'd repeated multiple times since then.

Brushing a dirt-covered hand across her forehead, Dorothy wiped away the beads of sweat that had collected, as best she could, and removed her sun hat. The hot ball of fire in the sky beat down against her tan skin as she watched Jimmy's car approaching from afar. In that moment, she wished so badly that Aunt Em was here. She had always been better at prolonging things than Dorothy.

The car came sputtering across the pebbled drive, past the wheat fields, and stopped in front of the foundation of the old porch. After the tornado had torn across everything with its windy paws, the rebuild hadn't gone easily, especially with the cost of supplies and labor. That had been the start of the farm's downfall.

As Jimmy stepped out from the car, she waited for her heart to speed up at the sight of him, wished she could make it thump harder. But she just couldn't fall in love with him, no matter how much he dreamed of her doing so, no matter how much she wanted to. He was nice and it would save her farm but the convenience would never be enough.

He took off his hat—displaying his neatly side-swept blond hair—and placed it at his chest while he moved toward her, as though he was prepared for a funeral. Dressed in an all-black suit, he seemed calm, but she noticed the rhythmic motions of his fingertips against his hat. She knew right then and there the news wasn't going to be good. It was a funeral, one for her home—a home she would have to leave, and never return to. She didn't know where she would go next. Back to the institution? That was where the town would try to send her anyway, even if Jimmy tried to stop them.

"Hello, Dorothy." Jimmy smiled, his pearly teeth shining under the sun.

"Hello, Jimmy." Dorothy tried to smile back, but she couldn't. Her heart did start pounding then, because she needed him to just spill the beans instead of hoarding them in his pocket.

Jimmy craned his neck and studied the pile of vegetables on the ground behind her. "You know you can't pluck all those carrots and save the farm." He wasn't being mean about it, only speaking the truth.

"I know." She sighed, taking a step closer to him so he could unharness the news.

"Then come with me." He dropped his hat on the grass and

10

grasped her hands with his warm fingers, his sky-blue eyes catching hers. "Marry me."

Dorothy hesitated, thought about saying yes, since that would make things better. But it wouldn't be fair to Jimmy because she didn't love him like that. She had never loved him in the way that two hearts should be drawn together. Instead she'd made mistakes in her desperation and done things she shouldn't have. With all her being, she didn't mean to hurt him. "You know I can't..."

"Who else are you going to find to take care of you?" His hand skimmed the side of her face, cradling it.

"Why?" Dorothy tore herself away from him. "Because everyone in town thinks of me as Crazy Dorothy?" She pressed her finger to his chest, jabbing it in as deeply as she could, not caring that it was un-lady like. It may have been the 1920s, but sometimes this town felt as if it was trapped in centuries past. "You think I'm crazy, don't you? Besides, I can handle myself just fine."

"I don't think you're crazy, Dorothy." He looked defeated while worry lines etched into his forehead. "I just think you've had a hard time. When we were kids, after the tornado, and you said you'd come back from a faerie world called Oz, you changed. But just because you think something is real, and it isn't, that doesn't make you crazy."

Perhaps the missing piece of why her heart could never be his was because he'd never once believed that maybe her story was true. "I still can't marry you. The right girl is waiting out there for you. I know it."

Jimmy didn't say a single word as he studied the ground.

She couldn't handle the silence any longer. "Now just break it to me. What's to become of the farm? Is there any saving it?"

He scooped up his hat from the ground and placed it gingerly back on, then silently pursed his lips and shook his head. "No. My father isn't keeping it or I could have tried harder. It's worth more to auction off to a buyer." Glenn was lead at the bank, and

Jimmy worked for him. But even with Jimmy pushing his father to help her out, it was no use. The farm was just in too much debt.

Reaching into his jacket pocket, he pulled out an off-white envelope and handed it to her. "I'm sorry, Dorothy. All it says is that the house will be claimed in two days. I really do wish my father would have listened to me." His hand pressed softly against her cheek again. "If you ever need a door open for you, mine will always be." He turned and walked away, his shoulders slumping a bit more than when he'd originally arrived.

"I'm sorry, too," she whispered to herself. Sorry he'd believed she would have loved him. Even then, she hated Glenn and wouldn't have wanted to see the man's face as her father-in-law. She silently hoped Jimmy would never turn out like his father, but something told her he'd always be a proper gentleman.

She watched the car back out and drive off, kicking up the dust of the road once more. She plummeted to her knees when she knew he could no longer see her. Dorothy should have asked Jimmy to stay with her a little longer, not as a lover, but a friend, the one who had always defended her in front of everyone. Yet Dorothy truly believed that deep, deep down in his heart, he thought her to be crazy, too. She wished *someone* believed her about her past.

Wicked Witch. Glinda. Slippers. Scarecrow. Lion. Tin Man. Emerald City. Home. She pressed her palms to her head and pushed as hard as she could, trying to shove away the thoughts of creatures that everyone told her weren't real. She screamed across the wheat and corn fields again and again until her voice cracked and her throat felt rough.

"It isn't real. It isn't real."

"It is real. It is real."

The silver slippers that had taken her back home hadn't been on her feet when she'd awoken ten years ago in the wheat field. If it was real, then where were they?

"Stop it!" But she couldn't control her spinning thoughts.

Leaving everything sprawled out across the ground, except for the shovel, she ran toward the house. Once she crossed the threshold, she stomped to the living room and smashed the shovel across the family portraits resting on the work bench, the paintings from the walls, the knickknacks on the shelves, then slammed the tool against the wooden table where no one ate but her. Fighting back her tears, Dorothy struck the wall, creating a large dent before tossing the shovel to the wood floor with a clang. "Why couldn't you two believe me?" she screamed to the ghosts of her aunt and uncle, wherever they were. "If you two loved me so much, then why couldn't you just listen to me!"

Dorothy didn't feel like eating, even though she'd slaughtered the last remaining pig that morning to prepare one final stew. Now, there were no animals left to worry about either. She'd sold all the chickens and cows in an attempt to save the farm. There was nothing left to sell anymore.

With heavy eyelids, she walked over broken glass and prepared a bath. She stripped herself of her dirty clothing and slumped down into the warm water. Closing her eyes, she repeated the words *there's no place like home*, until she drifted away, praying she would wake in the Land of Oz.

Something sounded, jolting Dorothy out of her deep dreamless world she'd entered. She'd fallen asleep in the bath—the water was no longer warm but freezing, her skin covered in gooseflesh.

The sound came again, a light tinkling of metal against metal. Snatching up a towel from the sink, she wrapped it around her wet body and hurried into her room. She tossed on a sleeveless white button-up shirt with a collar, paired with a clean set of striped overalls and black flats.

Remaining as quiet as possible, Dorothy fished out her uncle's rifle from beneath her bed. Numerous wolves had come on to the farm that she'd had to shoot so they wouldn't harm the other animals or destroy the crops. But this disturbance sounded different. There was always the chance of an intruder, too. Everyone in town knew "Crazy Dorothy" lived by herself out on the farm with no nearby neighbors. It would be so easy for someone to break into her house and take what little she had. But she had her rifle prepared, and because of Uncle Henry, she knew how to use it well.

The noise came again, out the window, somewhere in the wheat field. She scrambled to light a lantern as she opened the front door while holding the rifle awkwardly in the other hand. A sharp thrash echoed directly in the middle of the wheat, the tall stalks swaying with the wind under the silvery glow of the moon. This time, the noise was accompanied by a trickle of emerald green light, illuminating the wheat stalks. Flashing once, twice, and continuing as though it were signaling her to draw closer. She inhaled sharply, setting down the lantern. That brilliant green was something she knew all too well, despite the ten years that had passed since she'd been eleven.

"Oz," she whispered, almost dropping the rifle. "No, no. That can't be it." Aunt Em would be ashamed if Dorothy chose to believe, if she slipped down that yellow brick road of insanity again. After all the work Aunt Em had put in to reversing Dorothy's delusions.

Aunt Em was no longer there to make Dorothy think she could be wrong.

I could be right. I could have always been right.

Heart galloping in her chest, she took off toward the field, skirting around stalks of wheat, like she was eleven years old once again. Except the last time there was emerald illumination, she'd been inside of her house within a tornado. But that light had been there, too.

Right then, she would do anything for the yellow brick road to lead her anywhere else but here—instead of remaining in a world with nothing. She was supposed to be out of the house in

14

two days' time, but if she could find a way back to Oz—a place where no one thought of her as Crazy Dorothy—she would take the opportunity and not look back.

Pushing away tall and thin stalks of wheat, while avoiding the scurrying of mice feet, Dorothy followed the flickering light until, in front of her, there stood a green outline shimmering in the air, resembling a doorway.

"Dorothy," a male's deep voice called—one that was all-too familiar. "Dorothy, you need to come back. *Now.*"

It was real. It was real. It was real. She wished Aunt Em and Uncle Henry were alive to see this, to believe her. And she *wished* Toto was by her side, as he'd been the last time. But even her little dog had passed on to a new life.

Breathing in the night air and the heavy scent of her farm, she pressed her hand into the doorway and wiggled her fingers. She tugged her arm back and peered down at her palm. To see the land of Oz in all its glory, all she had to do was step through. With a smile she couldn't contain, Dorothy pressed her hand into the flickering green once more. Something roughly grasped her palm and yanked her within the portal, not leaving her enough time to scream or even yelp as she dropped her rifle in the dirt.

CHAPTER THREE

TIN

The moment a delicate hand came through the portal, Tin snatched the wrist and hauled the rest of the human into Oz. A human that was *supposed* to be Dorothy. Had he gotten the location wrong? He'd traveled far to reach the same dwarf-infested village she'd dropped into ten years ago, but this was distinctly *not* a little girl.

This was ... a woman. Wearing tight striped overalls that accentuated her curves and a white collared shirt that barely contained what was underneath. Her hair was dreadfully tousled and sopping wet from the shoulders down, but the wonder filling her eyes made something crack deep inside him. Tin threw her arm from his grasp, his lip curling in disgust at the thought.

"Oz." Her voice was barely audible as she slowly turned away from him, taking in the dwarf village.

He followed the mortal woman's eyes as they took in the decrepit town. Dozens of fire-lit posts highlighted the short, white buildings with round straw roofs. All the color in town came from the broken shutters, paint-chipped doors, and crooked flowerboxes, though it was difficult to see any of it at night. Stone paths led from each doorstep to the main square, which butted against the swirled end of the yellow and red brick roads. Where Dorothy's house had fallen on the Wicked Witch of the East stood a golden statue of the girl with a braid over each shoulder and, beside her, that wiry, four-legged creature she was so attached to.

"This is *Oz*," Dorothy said a bit louder.

"Where the hell else would it be?" Tin stepped in front of her, jaw clenched. "Who are you?"

"My name's—" Her eyes fell on his face for the first time and she gasped.

Tin grabbed the woman by the upper arms before she could run, screaming, and alert every fae in town. The iron tips of his gloves pricked her skin when he squeezed. "Who. Are. You?"

"Dorothy." She struggled to free herself but he held firm. "It's *me*, Tin. Dorothy. Now let go."

He scowled at her, and she scowled right back. There was no way this was the same human who'd destroyed the Wicked Witch of the West—Reva. The real Dorothy was at least a foot shorter with a rounder face and an overall naivety about her. The statue directly behind this fraud was a perfect likeness, from the ribbons holding her braided hair, right down to the ruffled socks on her feet.

"Imposter," Tin snarled.

"Of course it's me!" She fought against his grip again but only managed to dig the iron tips on his gloves deeper into her arms.

Tin glared menacingly. Mortals aged faster than the fae, but this progression seemed extreme. "That's Dorothy." He spun her around to face the dulled statue and pointed. "See the difference?"

She wrinkled her nose. "They made me into a monument?"

"Stop lying!" he roared.

"It's been ten years, you oaf!" she snapped. "I *grew up*. And

17

speaking of looking differently, what happened to your face?" Her lips parted as she studied him, seeming to grow concerned.

Tin released her as fast as one would drop a red-hot ember. Everyone knew what happened to his face—he had become a story parents told offspring to make them behave. *Do as I say or the Tin Man will snatch you from your bed.* It made sense this woman didn't know specifics, but she wouldn't ask what happened if she hadn't seen him before the branding.

"If you're Dorothy," he said carefully, "Where's your little rat, Tutu?"

Her eyes narrowed. "*Toto.*"

"That's what I said."

"My *dog* died, not that it's any of your business." She crossed her arms, the movement pushing up her cleavage. Tin couldn't stop his eyes from flicking downward. "You *are* Tin, aren't you?"

He held out his arms as if to say *who else would I be?* They were both quiet for a long moment before Dorothy broke the silence.

"That's impossible. The Tin I knew wasn't a self-righteous prick."

A surprised laugh burst from his chest. Tin leaned in closer, smelling the light scent of her soap, and cocked an eyebrow. "The fae you knew ten years ago wanted to be good."

"Which is why the Wizard broke the curse on your heart."

"An entirely useless organ. I'm glad it turned back to stone." He took in the statue of Dorothy again and considered the drastic change. Lion better not try to weasel out of payment, especially if Tin had to put up with her shit for very long. Lion's macabre lover wanted to wear Dorothy's head? Well, this was the only one Dorothy had. His gaze flicked back to the grown woman to find her staring, lips parted in horror at his revelation—an expression he was used to—and sighed.

"Your heart is stone again?" She gripped her chest as though he would rip her heart from beneath her ribcage to replace it with his.

There was nothing for her to worry about. He wouldn't

18

touch her fragile mortal organ. The Gnome King had done him a favor when he'd cursed Tin's parents—the Heartless Curse had turned his heart to stone in retaliation for the lack of mercy they'd shown the Gnome Queen. The queen had begged for their help to hide her from gremlin marauders but, understandably, his parents bolted their door shut instead. When the queen was cut down on the doorstep of Tin's childhood home, the king had needed someone to punish. Perhaps the avenging king wouldn't have cursed Tin's mother if he'd known Tin grew in her womb—damning an innocent child to the same fate—or if he'd found the gremlins responsible. He was grateful the Gnome King hadn't known because if the few short years with a beating heart had taught Tin anything, it was that emotions made a mess of everything. It was a welcomed event when Oz's magic wore off and his heart solidified again. Dorothy could keep her wretched thing thumping in her chest.

At least until Lion got ahold of her.

"And this fae doesn't give a fuck." Tin ground his teeth. "We have to get off the road before we're seen, unless you want to be ripped apart by the night beasts tonight."

Dorothy grew rigid and stayed silent. Finally, an action from her that pleased him.

She shifted her concerned gaze to the dwarves' lantern-lit homes. Each door was painted a different pastel color and the inn where Tin had already secured a room was no different. He gave her a small push toward the pink door at the edge of town. Unfortunately, he hadn't factored his strength—or her mortal body—into the motion, and Dorothy stumbled forward.

"What the hell?"

He winced at the volume of her voice. The last thing they needed was to wake the dwarves this time of night. There was no telling whether they would get cranky miners, peppy singers, or, gods forbid, someone who recognized the woman beside him.

"Apologies," he mumbled to quiet her. There was nothing

19

to be sorry for.

It seemed to pacify her despite the insincerity in his tone. "Where are the munchkins?"

"The mun—oh. Right. The dwarves." He'd forgotten Dorothy called them that.

She looked at him skeptically. "Glinda said they were munchkins."

"Glinda is an idiot," he snapped and tucked Dorothy into his side. She shifted away from him as he hid her beneath his cloak. Was she going to make everything difficult? This was why he preferred jobs that ended in blood. Heads didn't talk once they were removed. "Stop fussing. Oz isn't how you remember it."

Some residual trust must've lingered inside Dorothy because she relaxed into Tin and allowed him to lead her into the inn. They hurried through the closed tavern with the long liquid-stained tables, worn stools, and wooden steins hanging from hooks behind the bar. Small barrels rested on shelves, ready to be cracked when the tavern opened again the next night. The sound of shuffling feet in a back room had Tin hauling Dorothy upstairs to their room. Every squeak of the planked floor had him wincing, and he nearly had to bend in half to fit through the doorframes, but they made it all the way to the room without seeing anyone else. Langwidere expected Tin to deliver Dorothy within the next week, *alive*, so her head could be properly removed, but he needed to rest first. Not flee in the middle of the night.

The click of the lock seemed to mean something completely different to Dorothy, however. "Where's Glinda?" Without waiting for an answer, she asked, "Why isn't Oz how I remember it? And what happened to your heart?"

Gods. Will this girl shut the hell up already?

Once his cloak was folded on the chair, he lifted his axe from his waist and tucked the head of the weapon beneath his pillow. The room was almost too warm, the bed too soft, and the ceiling too low, but it was more comfortable than the forest floor. Tin

20

pulled his shirt off next, along with his gloves, and tossed the black fabric over the painted statue of a young Dorothy that sat on the nightstand. A vase of red flowers tipped, spilling water all over the floor, but that was fine with him. There were more on the windowsill, dresser, and round table anyway. He flopped down on top of the bed covers without sparing Dorothy a word.

The weight of Dorothy's stare on his abdomen made his muscles flex involuntarily. If she asked about the handful of scars decorating his skin, he wouldn't lie. The jagged one on his side came from an ogre, and the puckered circle on his shoulder from a poisoned spear. He couldn't remember where he got other smaller ones, but the important thing was that every wound ended with a big, fat payday. Something told Tin that Dorothy wouldn't appreciate hearing how his new profession was murder.

"See something you like?" he asked with a lazy grin. She blushed bright red. Tin yawned, satisfied with her reaction, and shut his eyes. The silver key to their shared room was securely in his right pants' pocket, which meant Dorothy was securely in his grasp. They would leave at dawn, after the dwarves settled into their routines for the day, to avoid unnecessary attention.

"Tin!"

He cracked one eye to find Dorothy flushed with anger. "Are you really not going to tell me anything?"

"I don't see why any of it matters," he grumbled. She made a choked noise. "Fine. If it will get you to shut up. Glinda hasn't come out of the South in years. She's too busy doing whatever it is she does. My heart is my business. Oz isn't the same because the Wizard is a faerie fruit addicted fool who left the Emerald City, which is now in chaos. And you're back because I opened a portal and *brought you here*. The last bit was rather exhausting though, so do me a favor and stop talking."

"But—"

"At the very least, try not to draw attention to us by gawking out the window or stomping around like an angry troll."

His cloak landed hard on his face. "Call me a troll again,"

Dorothy snarled.

Tin blinked in surprise at her audacity before using the cloak as a blanket. "An *angry* troll. And you just proved my point."

"We haven't seen each other in ten years, you pull me back to Oz, and then want to take a nap?" she asked, indignant.

"Let's get one thing clear, shall we?" His piercing silver eyes latched onto her brown ones. "I don't care. Not about old times, not about you. This is a job."

"Job?"

"Lion hired me to bring you to him." If he left out the part about Lion's courage driving him into darkness, and into the bed of that crazy bitch Langwidere, Dorothy wouldn't know to be wary of her old friend. She would follow Tin straight to Langwidere's door for the tradeoff. "He needs your help." *To keep his lover happy and swimming in new heads.*

"Is he okay? What does he need help with?"

"Dorothy," Tin warned.

"What about Crow?"

He rolled over and gave Dorothy his back. The truth was, Tin had no idea what had happened to Crow after the Wizard got his brain working properly, but if he had to guess, it wasn't good. Nothing was anymore.

Chapter Four

Dorothy

Dorothy stood in the darkened night of a strange, utterly small room with a low ceiling that her head almost brushed against, that Tin's *had* touched. While the sun had already set in her world, it had also found its hiding place here.

Her breathing increased with growing annoyance as she watched the fae in front of her, the moonlight highlighting the silver of his long hair.

When she'd first realized that Tin was the one who'd pulled her through the portal, she couldn't help being overjoyed. But that had quickly slipped away when it had become apparent that he wasn't the same person.

And now, he thought he could just roll over and turn his back on her? Wearing a cloak like a blanket? That she would be fine and dandy about it? Outrageous. She stomped to the other side of the bed, not bothering to placate him with silence. But as soon as her gaze took in the markings on his cheek again, her anger left her. Where had the silver lines come from? And how was he already asleep? Her feet clomping the wood hadn't disrupted him in the slightest, as his breaths came out slow and even.

She'd noted as she'd peered under the tall fiery posts, at the houses with chipped paint and broken pieces, that this wasn't the Oz she remembered. This wasn't the Tin she remembered either. Everyone had been happy-go-lucky before, besides the witch and her minion monkeys. But she hadn't come across anyone else yet either, so perhaps the rest of Oz wasn't as gloomy as this outer layer.

When she'd last been in Oz with Tin and the others, he'd been quiet and sulky, but nothing like this. It was as though he was jaded now. And when his stone heart had become a live, beating organ, he'd even cracked a smile at her before she'd left. That perfect smile had remained with her while back in Kansas, the one she'd always sworn to herself that she'd see again. There were no smiles now.

He'd told her Lion needed her. If she couldn't get answers from Tin tonight, well, she'd leave him behind and go find her other friend. She wasn't going to waste her time here. And maybe once she found Lion, he could tell her where Crow was.

"Sorry, Tin, you can catch up with me if you so desire," she whispered to herself, and made way for the door, this time keeping her feet silent.

Only, she found the door locked when she tried to turn the knob. She narrowed her eyes with the discovery that it needed a key to exit from inside. Her gaze drifted back to the sleeping fae.

She'd seen him stow his axe—his prized possession—beneath the pillow, but nothing else. Her one chance of leaving had to be on his body, and she had a feeling he wouldn't hand it over to her willingly.

Dorothy tiptoed back to the bed, her eyes lingering on the rise of his naked chest where a portion of his cloak had slipped away. No key would be found there. In fact, she didn't know how he wasn't getting chilly with all that exposed skin in the cold room.

24

Reaching forward, she softly padded her hands down the sides of his cloak, finding only emptiness. As her eyes drifted to his pants, her face heated at where her hands would have to venture next.

Taking a deep swallow that felt too loud in her ears, she slipped her fingertips inside his right pocket. *Ah-ha.* Something metal brushed along her digits. Just as she was about to pull it out, two firm and warm hands grasped both her wrists, preventing her escape.

"I don't think so," Tin growled in a low whisper.

Before she could respond, her fingers were ripped from his pocket—key long gone from her grasp—and her body shoved up against his with an arm planted at her waist. All 'snug and cozy,' except she knew his intentions were anything but.

"Apparently," he murmured by her ear, his breath warm and tickling her nape, "you're not to be trusted. Goodnight."

There was no goodnight.

Grunting, she wiggled and tried to roll over to face him, but he was too strong. So she settled on talking to the grimy windowpane instead of his face. "Before, you mentioned that Lion needs me. I think we should go now. No need to sleep."

He didn't answer. If anything, he seemed to hold onto her tighter.

Huffing, she turned her head over her shoulder, unable to see anything in the dark now that the moonlight had shifted. "Can you at least answer why we need to stay here?"

He exhaled with agitation, and even without seeing him, she knew he was scowling. "I don't think you want to venture out into Oz at this time of night. As I said, things aren't as they once were."

She'd traveled through the night before. The last time she was here, she remembered holding on to Crow's hand for a good bit of the journey. He may not have been able to talk very clearly most of the time, but she'd felt closest to him, like he was her protector. As for Tin, there'd been a different feeling about him, one she hadn't been able to name back then, one she was no longer feeling now. And Lion, while being a big baby, had done the best he could.

Dorothy wished she hadn't dropped her shotgun on the way into the portal. She wished she had Toto who would bark and scare the things of this world. But now it was only her and this man who wasn't really a man at all.

"Tell me why then," she said. "Why can't we leave now?"

He didn't answer.

"Tin." She hated that his name came out more of a plea.

"Stop saying that."

"What?" Her brows lowered in confusion. "Your name?"

"Calling me by name would mean we're friends, and we're not that. Not anymore."

"But—"

He let out a grumble as if he was warring with himself before he finally added, "If we left now, you'd have wished you stayed, so trust me on this. I told you earlier, there are night beasts here."

Dorothy couldn't help wanting to spew out more questions about what kind of night beasts, but he was already asleep again. Something told her to listen to him, especially when crackling sounds outside stirred. She lifted her head an inch and listened. It wasn't the chanting of the munchkins in song—*dwarves*—it was something far more sinister. Low growls and gurgles seemed to swarm the town. *It must be the night beasts Tin mentioned.*

A shiver ran up her spine and she closed her eyes, curling closer into Tin, even though she should have moved farther away. As the sounds grew louder and louder, she was grateful the bed was far too narrow for him to push her away. He may not consider her a friend anymore, but she still considered him one as she remembered his smile to her, from long ago, once more.

Her farm was no longer hers, and regardless of the changes to this place, she wanted to stay in Oz. Same as the last time she was here, she would make things better again. How bad could it truly be?

A yawn escaped her and her eyes fluttered before she drifted off to sleep, pressed tightly against Tin's arm.

Something hard nudged Dorothy's shoulder. "Sleeping," she said, knowing it was Tin. He'd had his terms last night on when to sleep. This time, things would be on *her* terms of when to wake up.

The nudge came again, harder than before. She flicked open her eyes, meeting that of a bare chest with a few pale scars running up it. Tin's chest was firm and ripped, and nothing like Jimmy's flat chest and stomach. She quickly tore her gaze away and focused on the wooden handle of the axe poking at her arm.

Narrowing her eyes, she drifted her gaze up to Tin's face, catching on his silver irises. He was scowling at her, and she found herself unsurprised by his expression.

"You could have just said, 'Dorothy, it's time to leave.' You know, like a gentleman would do."

"I'm no gentleman." Tin tugged his shirt on and placed his cloak around his shoulders.

"That you aren't," she muttered and sat on the edge of the bed, reaching her hands up, and arching her back forward to pop it. The farm work the day before had done a number on her body. The sky out the window appeared bright, and whatever beastly noises had erupted through the night were gone now.

"What are you doing?" Tin asked, observing her as if she was a species he'd never seen before.

"Can I not stretch for a moment?"

"No," he grunted, turning around and heading for the door.

Rolling her eyes, she hurried after him as he unlocked it with a silver key.

"What's for breakfast?" she asked as she followed him down the narrow hallway with its bare, sickly-green walls, to the stairs on the first floor. The room stood empty except for a dwarf with spiraled gray hair, seated at the front desk.

"Whatever you find on the way." Tin didn't look back at her as he slammed the key down in front of the dwarf.

"Hi, I'm—"

Tin wrapped a hand over her mouth. "Leaving. She's leaving." He pushed her through the door and out toward the yellow brick road. Tired of his coldness already, she bit his hand and he cursed, quickly removing it.

"What was that about?" she asked.

"Don't mention your name to anyone, understand?" He shook his hand out then balled it into a fist. "It's dangerous."

"I'm not fae. People can call me Dorothy Gale all they want, and I can't be controlled." She wondered what Tin's full name was, but she knew he would never tell her. And if he did, she'd control him right then.

He sighed. "Everyone knows what you did before, and while a lot are happy about it, some aren't. You'll eventually understand why."

Dorothy took a deep swallow, as she peered at the unkempt village, wondering how defeating the Wicked Witch of the West would make people unhappy. "But—"

"That's enough."

She could tell he was in no mood to say anything else on that matter. "Fine, but I really do need something to eat." Her stomach twisted and turned—it had been without anything since early the day before.

With a frustrated shake of the head, he pointed to a fruit tree up the road.

She narrowed her eyes. "I can't eat faerie fruit." Crow had warned her what it did to mortals, and apparently, the Wizard was addicted to it. Even when she'd met him, he hadn't seemed completely sane, so perhaps he was back then too.

"Mmm, too bad then."

She scowled.

He pointed again toward the trees. "There are some past

those with various nuts."

"Thank you."

"Don't thank me."

Dorothy stepped onto the yellow brick road and stared at the withering houses as she passed. Her heart beat rapidly as she gathered nuts into the pockets of her overalls while stepping on several to crack them open.

Tin ate a few, then bit into a luscious-looking piece of fruit before they started back down the yellow path toward the South. The breeze held a tinge of coolness as it blew around them. The trees shuffled and swayed as Dorothy watched brownies and faeries swarm around the yellow and orange fruit.

As they trekked farther and farther away from Dwarf Country, where only forestry surrounded them, something wobbled beneath her feet, catching her off balance.

She peered down and gasped at the cracked, shifted rectangular pieces. "What happened to the yellow brick road?"

Tin only shook his head and continued walking past her.

"What happened?" Dorothy asked again. The road was not only a faded yellow now but there were cracks, some broken bricks, others missing, as though a tornado had run itself across the once beautiful path.

"Most of the Emerald City and outlying areas have been destroyed." He shrugged with nonchalance. "None of the territories are what they used to be."

"But not Glinda's, right? The South is okay, isn't it?" It couldn't be that bad if that was where they were headed, could it?

He paused. "You ask too many questions. That's where we're headed because that's where Lion is."

"I defeated the Wicked Witch of the West. My house landed on the Wicked Witch of the East. Things should be better." There was Locasta of the North and Glinda of the South. Both were good and both had planned to share the territories that the wicked had held.

"Once a villain dies, another always rises. Good doesn't always conquer evil. Besides, why do you care? You left Oz and never looked back."

She grasped his arm and spun him around, her anger boiling. "I never stopped looking back! I went home, Tin. But that didn't mean I didn't ever want to return! I couldn't! No one ever came to me, I never found another portal, and the people in my world didn't believe me. I was locked away for months at a time. People hurt me, physically and emotionally. Do you even know what that's like?"

His expression slipped for a moment, only briefly, but it was there. He'd looked as though he wanted to give a full answer, but then he simply said, "No."

"That's right, because you have a heart of stone." Her nostrils flared.

"And you are but a lowly mortal." He shrugged and walked away.

Her anger rose, and she clenched her fists. She would head to the South by herself, but not before she forced him to show some emotion.

She lunged forward, yanked the axe from his grip, and took off with a heavy sprint. It may have been childish to steal his weapon, but she didn't care. He was irritating her to no end.

Behind her, the pound of his feet reverberated, but she was quickly gaining space between them. Then a body slammed into her from the side, knocking her to the ground. She released hold of the axe and shouted in Tin's face, "You're the new coward! Somehow since I've been gone, you've inherited Lion's old ways."

But it wasn't Tin's silver irises she was looking at; it was something else, with reddened eyes and saliva dripping from its mouth. A man with rotting skin and clumps of hair missing— mortal—one who had eaten too much faerie fruit.

As the man snapped his teeth down toward her face, the slice of a weapon came across his neck. The head vanished and hot blood sprayed Dorothy.

All that remained was a headless body slumped on her chest, warm blood pooling out from the dead man's neck.

Strong hands yanked Dorothy up by her arms, the still body falling from her. Two silver eyes met hers, blazing with fury.

"I told you Oz isn't the same," Tin said through gritted teeth. "Now, are you going to listen to me?"

She quickly nodded, even though it wasn't entirely true, but right then she would.

Chapter Five

Tin

—————◆——————◆—————

Humans and fae didn't have much in common, but neither seemed to listen to sense. Apparently, Dorothy was one of them—even if she had just agreed to start. With a snarl on his lips, Tin stared down at the blood-soaked woman. The faerie fruit addict's body sprawled at their feet, his head tossed aside, and his blood coating Dorothy's face. He had expected her to cry or scream. It was good she hadn't. Little was worse than getting a mouthful of blood, especially that of a mortal addicted to faerie fruit. Something about the fruit made it disgustingly bitter. He'd found that out the hard way, completely by accident, when he'd assassinated a human at the beginning of his career in exchange for a week of room and board. He should've expected a good amount of blood to spurt from the thing's neck and stood to the side, but live and learn... More dangerous for Dorothy, the blood carried a scant trace of the fruit's addictive properties.

"Are you sure you're going to listen now?" Tin growled at Dorothy. "Because it will make saving you repeatedly a real hassle if you don't have any coin."

Dorothy shook in his grip, undoubtedly from the shock settling in, mixed with fury. "You'd charge me to save my life?"

"I charge per kill." It was double the price if a client charged headfirst into trouble and made things more difficult. Tin released her to settle his bloody axe back on his hip. They would stop at the first body of water to wash off the weapon and their filth before the scent attracted fae beasts. "Since you didn't know that, and given our history, there's no charge for this one."

She had to be delivered to Lion and Langwidere *alive* for him to cash in—a payment he deserved ten times over already—but Dorothy didn't need to know that. A good dose of fear had the potential to keep her in line.

When Dorothy simply stood there, staring at the decapitated body, Tin scraped moss off a nearby tree. "Here. Use this before any of the blood gets in your mouth."

She snatched the moss from his palm and lowered her brows. "How is this supposed to help?"

"Wipe your face with it," he instructed. Dorothy dropped the moss to the ground and used her hands instead, which only smeared the blood more. Tin shook his head in disdain. "Use the moss like a cloth."

"This is fine for now." She wiped her hands on her thighs.

"You'd rather risk a faerie fruit high than use the moss?" he asked in disbelief.

Her eyes flicked up to his for a moment, almost as if she was gauging whether he was serious, before scooping the moss up from the ground. "Thanks."

He hadn't given it to her for thanks. He gave her the moss to cut down on the smell and risk of contamination. Though, if he was being honest with himself, the contamination didn't matter much. He was delivering her to Langwidere, after all.

"Did I get it all?" Dorothy asked after scrubbing her face. The blood stained her skin light pink, but the moss effectively collected a majority of the mess.

"Mostly."

She reached for the same tree Tin had taken the moss from. He watched her struggle to scrape more than tiny bits and pieces off, amused at her effort, before using his iron-tipped gloves to rip a larger patch free. "Allow me."

Dorothy stretched for the fresh moss, but Tin swung his arm out of reach. The worried gleam in her eyes made Tin smirk. Without another word, he had the moss to Dorothy's jaw line where a large streak of blood remained. She gasped as he pulled it slowly from her ear toward her chin and the sound caused a crumbling sensation behind his ribs.

For a mortal woman, she wasn't unattractive. Langwidere would be pleased with her delicate features. Though, admittedly, in a different way than it pleased him. He'd taken pleasure from a few masochistic thrill-seekers over the years, but he never knew their names. Dorothy was different. Wondering what expression she would wear in the throes of passion wasn't an idea Tin should entertain. Ever. And yet, the desire to touch her burned sudden and deep. Having her firmly against him in such a small bed all night didn't help either. She was so warm, so trusting, as she pressed her soft body against him, filling his senses with her feminine aroma. It lingered even now, and Tin's cock stiffened. Would she taste as good as she smelled?

He jerked away from Dorothy in frustration. "Good enough to keep us alive until we hit the river."

"Excuse me?" she asked, slightly breathless but recovering quickly. "What do you mean, keep us alive?"

Tin held his arms out to signal the forest. "I mean, all the pixies, kobolds, and leprechauns who call these woods home. If you thought the addict was bad…"

He let the threat linger in hopes of further ensuring her obedience, but they weren't likely to be attacked by any of those fae. Others would, but occasionally his reputation worked in his favor. It was the trolls they had to avoid. The kelpies at the river still had it out for him after he'd butchered one to use the scales for his clothes. Both were manageable threats though, and he *did* need Dorothy to walk through the forest. He had no intention of carrying her if she became too frightened, and there wasn't time to walk around the forest before Lion's deadline.

"Shall we try this again?" Tin asked.

Dorothy nodded, then quickly shook her head. "One minute," she mumbled as she ran back to the headless body. She bent over him and carefully plucked a small knife from where it was tucked inside one of his boots. Blade clutched to her chest, Dorothy hurried back to Tin's side.

"You don't need that," he told her. He would protect her until she was with Lion.

Dorothy pointed to the bloody scene behind her. "I disagree."

"Fine." He drew a deep breath and pushed it out sharply. "Let's get moving."

He didn't wait for her to respond before turning on his heel and marching forward. For a moment he worried she wouldn't follow and he would be forced to drag her the entire way south. His fingers curled into fists, his ears straining to hear her. Maybe it *would* be faster—carrying her. An annoyed grunt left Tin's throat and the soft padding of Dorothy's footsteps sounded behind him.

By the time Tin and Dorothy arrived at the river bank, he was ready to toss her to the kelpies himself. She hadn't said a word since they began their journey a second time, but Tin was acutely aware of all the things she wasn't saying. He felt the unspoken words squeezing him like a vise.

Something was holding her back from saying whatever it was she had on her mind and Tin didn't care what that thing was. He was glad she wasn't asking the hard questions, glad he didn't have to explain. Gladder still that he didn't have to lie to her about Lion's intentions. His meeting with Lion a few nights ago was surprising, even to Tin. He had thought he'd heard it all from his clients, but procuring a former friend for decapitation as a *gift*? Lion's lover, Langwidere, would wear Dorothy's head well, just as she wore the dozens already in her possession. The head of a mortal child had seemed a strange choice when Lion had asked Tin to bring Dorothy back to Oz and lead her to Langwidere's doorstep alive, but it made sense now. Dorothy was already aging so rapidly. Her life wouldn't be cut short too prematurely. Besides, the pay was undeniably good.

Tin bent at the water's edge and dunked his hands beneath the liquid. After scanning the surface of the river for signs of life, he looked over his shoulder at the silent woman. Her cheeks were flushed and her chest rose and fell a little too quickly. He stood and studied her.

"Are you ill?"

"What?" she asked breathlessly.

He narrowed his eyes as if it would help him see what ailed her. Would it change things? Could Langwidere still utilize the head if she was sick? If not, they would have to treat the sickness themselves. Alive was alive—Lion never mentioned her health. "You look ill."

"I'm *tired*. Do you know what tired is?"

"We've only been traveling a few hours, and I've kept a slow pace for your mortal legs."

She scowled at him. "My *mortal legs* are significantly shorter than yours. I've practically had to sprint to keep up with you."

Tin blinked in surprise as his gaze fell to her legs. They were shorter, yes, but seemed perfectly capable of matching his pace. "What would you have me do? Crawl to Lion?"

"Yes. Crawl. It might give you back some of the humility you lost when your heart turned back into stone," she snapped.

"Clean yourself," he spat before he could dignify that with a response. It wouldn't be long until he never had to deal with her or her smart mouth again. He tugged the axe from his hip and Dorothy scrambled back a step. "Relax. I'm not going to hurt you."

Dorothy stood until Tin turned away from her and began cleaning the blood from his weapon, then joined him. He watched her splash water on her face from the corner of his eyes. It soaked the hair around her face, the strands clinging to her cheeks and forehead. Beads of water ran down her neck. Tin's gaze inadvertently fixed on the liquid drops as they raced further down into her cleavage, as he continued to shine the same spot on his axe, though it was no longer dirty. She moved on to her clothes—scrubbing at the stains with a rock and splashing water onto the fabric until the bright red faded to a muted pink. The white shirt Dorothy had on beneath her overalls hid *nothing* when wet. All he needed was to glimpse something he shouldn't when his malehood was already in revolt, so he turned his attention to his weapon.

When he looked up again, it was to find Dorothy staring at him and, for the first time in years, he wished he could hide his face. The blackened rings of bone held his silver locks tightly in place, however, showcasing his iron mutilation. Heavens above, what was he doing? Clearly, he'd gone too long without a female. When this job was finished, he needed a good fuck. It might take a while to find a brothel willing to serve him, but he'd pay an exorbitant price for their worst girl if that was what it took.

"I know it's none of my business, but will you tell me what happened to your face, Tin?" Dorothy asked in a quiet, thoughtful voice.

Tin sighed. "What does it matter?"

"It matters a lot." The tacky mud along the riverbank squished when she stood and came closer to him. "Tell me who *I* need to kill, because I don't think you did this to yourself."

He stiffened at her words. The thought of Dorothy killing anyone made him irrationally protective of her and her still-pure heart. He didn't understand why. Besides, his truth would change her opinion of him, and he wasn't sure he wanted that. It wasn't that Tin was ashamed of the events leading up to the Wizard's

37

punishment. He rarely felt anything more than anger and resignation since his heart hardened again, but if Dorothy knew what he was… If she knew he was an assassin—the *best* assassin in Oz—she would look at him like everyone else did. It would also lead to suspicions he couldn't afford. Lion could've hired anyone with knowledge of portals to bring Dorothy back if it was a friendly visit.

But he didn't. He'd hired Tin.

Tin, whose resume boasted thousands of kills and a distinct lack of morals, was once Dorothy's friend. They'd bonded as they traveled the yellow brick road together with Lion and Crow. If Oz had managed to truly break the Heartless Curse placed on Tin by the Gnome King, Lion's coin wouldn't weigh down his pocket now. But it *hadn't* worked. Lion knew that—all of Oz knew—which was likely why Lion hired Tin specifically.

If Lion's lover lopped off Dorothy's pretty little head and wore it as if it was her own, what was it to Tin? Nothing. So what if Langwidere continued terrorizing the South while pretending to be the savior of Oz?

"The Wizard did it," he said before he could stop himself. What did it matter if he told Dorothy how he was branded? She wouldn't be around long enough for it to make a difference and he could leave out certain details. So, he took a cloth from his bag to dry his axe and continued, "I was convicted of murder after the curse returned. Before that, I was one of the Wizard's bodyguards, so he let me off easy. Instead of having me publicly executed, he poured a single drop of molten iron upon me for each life I took."

Dorothy's eyes grew impossibly wide. "How many fae did you kill?"

Tin finished drying his axe, stood, and put the sharp blade back at his hip. "I didn't stick around to count. Dozens by then, I suppose. The eleven lords were what got me caught, though."

"But…" She paused, and Tin tried to read the mixture of horrified emotions on her face. It was impossible. "Oz would never do something so horrible to anyone!"

He scoffed. Dorothy had to be the only person in Oz—in *all* the fae lands—who would doubt the Wizard punished Tin. There had nearly been a riot when he wasn't sentenced to death. "Do you really want those answers, Dorothy? You won't like them."

"Of course I want the answers!"

Tin stepped closer and leaned down, perhaps too close, to give her a good look at the shining metal on his cheek. Past the blood still coating her clothing, a lingering scent of her soap mixed with his own scent from the night before struck his nostrils. Dorothy's eyes seemed to trace over each twisting path of iron. His skin had burned around the iron, and had never stopped. Burned and burned and burned until his only option was to embrace the pain. It was the ever-present ember that kept his rage smoldering even on his best day.

"One night, I left a gaming hall in the capital slightly inebriated and found the owner's son harassing a female outside. It didn't seem wrong to snap his neck—it still doesn't seem wrong. He deserved his fate. The female, less so, but she refused to stop screaming."

He stopped then. Stopped and waited for Dorothy to do the same. After hearing that story, the only sane response would be to run. Instead, she looked at him with pity, and there was nothing worse than that.

"I burned down the entire gambling hall afterward," he said to erase her expression. "If anyone tried to escape the inferno, I took them down with my axe. And that was only the beginning."

Tin had no idea what had come over him that night. The two deaths outside had been warranted, but not the rest. The Wizard should've had him killed for that first act—it would've saved a lot of lives. Since Oz had granted *mercy* though, Tin had schooled himself. He may not have a heart anymore, but that didn't mean he wanted to die. Murderous rampages were only tolerated if the coin purse was heavy enough now.

"Terrified of me yet?" he asked with a sneer. "Don't worry. You're safe as long as you're with me. Lion is paying me to deliver you alive and well. Finish getting cleaned up. I'll be just a few trees away."

Dorothy bit down on her bottom lip and met his gaze. Instead of fear, Tin found sorrow. Pity, as it turned out, wasn't the worst look he could receive.

Chapter Six

Dorothy

Exhaustion had taken over Dorothy's whole body from traveling—her slip-on shoes had done nothing except cause her feet to hurt. What she needed were boots like Tin wore, but it wasn't as if there was a store right around the corner in the middle of nowhere. Only fruit trees and a broken brick road surrounded them.

After washing the remainder of the blood and grime from herself as best she could at the river, she and Tin kept heading south, only stopping when he slayed something for them to eat. He remained quiet—she remained inquisitive. The world around her was broken … like Tin … like her, even the trees appeared melancholic, with their drooping branches. Tin wasn't the same fae she'd once known. He was a murderer, but he was what he was because this place had turned him that way.

Should she hate him? Yes. Was she frustrated with him? Yes. Did she feel pity for him? Yes…

Dorothy knew Tin wanted to take her to Lion, and the fae had been desperate enough to pay another to bring her to him.

Perhaps Lion was cowardly once more, or he would have come for her himself. This was all the Wizard's fault for making them believe that happiness could be permanent, that by her returning home everything would be perfect—it wasn't.

After she reunited with Lion, how would she even be able to help him? Dorothy no longer had the sparkling silver slippers to provide her with magic.

In the distance, something achingly familiar caught her attention, making her heart thump wildly: a city—the Emerald City. Lion... Tin... What she needed was someone else, someone who was braver than anyone she knew. *Crow.* He'd said he would remain in the city, that he'd needed to think about things.

Dorothy whirled to the side at the thought of Crow, almost gripping one of Tin's strong arms, absently wondering how firm it would feel beneath her fingertips... She shook away the thought and kept her minimal distance.

"I think I have an idea for our next step," Dorothy said with a wide smile, knowing that somewhere in the city her good friend waited.

Slowly, his demeanor dangerous, Tin halted and turned to face her, his silver eyes hard, his brows becoming one. "What are you talking about now?"

"I think instead of us going straight to the South, we should head to the Emerald City first." As Dorothy gazed in the distance, her smile dropped as the dying light highlighted the city. Like everything else she'd encountered, a sky-scraping tower appeared, crumbled in half. "What happened to the capital?" she whispered. Tin had told her everything was a mess, but she hadn't expected this.

"We aren't going anywhere else." He stepped toward her, close, closer, incredibly close. "The same thing happened there that's happened everywhere. A measly knife won't save you either. Oz left the Emerald City for who knows where, and Locasta and her beasts have claimed the eastern and northern

42

territories. She's battling for the Emerald City to be hers, too."

"Locasta? But she's good." Lion and Tin had both told her Locasta was good, like Glinda.

"Sometimes things change." He shrugged as though he didn't care, as if he didn't have a heart. Which, she supposed, he didn't since it had hardened back up.

"What about the West? Who has it since the Wicked Witch of the West is dead?"

He shrugged again. "Another fae like Locasta."

Dorothy remembered what Oz had done to Tin—she now knew he'd given Tin a heart that wasn't permanent. Lion didn't have his courage any longer. But what about Crow? What if he'd lost his brain, too? Unless their curses were different and his was really broken. But what if it wasn't? He was wiser than any of them when he was at full capacity. Even when he'd spoken in nonsensical riddles, Crow had somehow known how to keep her safe when she was just a young girl.

Not one to back down, Dorothy stepped as close as she could get and peered up at Tin. "I'm still going to leave and search for Crow there. Maybe someone has answers. If you don't want to come, then once I find him, we can meet you and Lion in the South. Then we'll head straight to Glinda. I know she can help us." Glinda might have been bubbly at times, but she knew fae magic better than anyone. And perhaps Glinda could also help Tin ... help him to restore his heart. As Dorothy stared at his face, at the hard silver ripples on his left cheek, she knew the scar still hurt. It didn't bother her to look at him. He was still beautiful, just as he was when he'd smiled at her before she'd left. But there was no smile now, hadn't been for a long time.

"No." Tin's answer sounded final.

Dorothy drew in a sharp breath and narrowed her eyes. "What do you mean *no*?"

"No." And there that word was again...

"Is this because of the payment?" she asked. "Lion will understand."

"No."

"Then I'm sorry, but we'll have to part ways for now. I promise I'll meet you in the South as soon as I can." She'd traveled by herself here before, then she'd stumbled upon Crow first. Perhaps she hadn't been alone because she'd had Toto, but she'd been by herself on her farm for quite some time. She may not have been able to save that, but she could try and help Tin by locating the silver slippers.

Dorothy knew what was about to come out of his mouth would be argumentative, but his eyes turned to the darkening sky and he released a string of curses. "I don't have time for this."

"I don't care—"

"The Emerald City is a wreck—I doubt Crow's even still there. So shut your mouth." Tin lifted her up from the ground. She gasped when he threw her over his shoulder as if she weighed nothing.

"I swear to God, I'm going to scream if you don't put me down right this instant!" She beat her fists against his hard back, but he didn't even seem fazed.

"Be quiet!" he growled in a low and deadly voice. "The sun is going down."

"And?" She wiggled her hips, trying to slip from his grasp. It didn't work.

"Like last night, the night beasts are going to come out soon." He moved off the broken yellow bricks toward the edge of the forest. "We don't have time to make it to another inn. Do you know whose fault that is? Yours. For traveling at a glacial pace and then starting this ridiculous discussion about searching for Crow, a fae who has been absent for years."

What she needed was her rifle. All she had was the small blade she'd swiped from the now-headless man who'd became addicted to faerie fruit. It was better for him to be dead than what he'd become.

"I don't care what you say," Dorothy seethed. "In the morning, I'm going to find Crow. He can shift—he'd be more help to Lion than I'd ever be."

"No."

When she was here last, she'd led the way, been the one in charge, but she'd taken everyone's thoughts into consideration. When had he decided to not listen to anyone but himself?

In the distance, a stirring sounded, a loud beating of wings. Then came the hooting, the growling, the ear-piercing screams, all from the Emerald City. While being outdoors this time, the noises clearer, she was able to recognize the sounds of the beasts. The minions had once belonged to the Wicked Witch, but they were now here. Why hadn't they chosen to rule themselves after the Wicked Witch died instead of flock to another? Dorothy lifted her head from Tin's back and watched in horror as the little bit of shining light filtered across a dull sparkle of green building wrapped in dead vines.

Before she could see the beasts clearly, Tin tossed them both to the ground. He threw his cloak around them. "Cradle your legs around my hips and hold me as close as you can."

"*What?*" Dorothy asked, horrified at the thought. She hadn't even had her legs that tightly around Jimmy the times they'd been together.

"Damn it, just do it—we're not fucking," he spat. "If you don't want to die out here, listen. If we stay hidden, they won't find us."

Getting ripped apart by flying monkeys with long talons, fangs, and thorned tails wasn't something she would wish for. Chest heaving, Dorothy heard the noisy rustling of the beasts drawing closer. Thankfully, she wasn't wearing a dress this time as she folded her legs around Tin's narrow waist and her arms around his warm neck.

He hurriedly adjusted his cloak and unlatched secret panels to make the cloth larger, then stretched it to fully cover them both. His arms seemed to hesitate for a split-second before they took hold around her. She could feel his soft breaths at her scalp just as he probably felt her rapid ones at his throat. An earthy scent enveloped her.

Dorothy's heart pounded as the growling and heavy flapping of wings boomed above them. The crashing of the monstrous things swarmed between branches, through leaves, colliding with the wind. Her grip on Tin tightened, even though she was still frustrated with him, even though she wanted to leave him behind and search for Crow. But he was keeping her safe. No matter what, she knew he was keeping her safe because he was still her friend—even a stone-hearted one. Just as she would keep him safe—once she broke his curse with Glinda and Crow's help.

The sounds faded, lighter and lighter, until they'd completely died down. Dorothy tried to inch backward, but Tin only held her tighter.

"It's fine now," she whispered at his ear.

"It's *not* fine." His voice came out raspy. "The beasts have watchers everywhere at night. There could even be one in the tree right above us."

She shuddered at the thought. "But can't they hear us?"

"No, that's why we need to stay put. The fae magic of my cloak will protect us."

"How did you come across such a thing? You didn't have it before." When she'd first found him, all he'd had was a rusted axe, a stone in his chest, and worn clothing. He'd even been without boots. The thought of that poor, once-optimistic fae made her chest tighten.

"You ask too many questions," he grumbled against her hair.

"And I'll ask more. Where did you get it?"

"I stole it from Oz. He'd stolen it from a witch."

"I'd say I think he deserved it." Oz had pretended to be a wizard, and he'd only been a man. She should have known to never trust him.

Tin chuckled, but then he interrupted it with a light cough as though he didn't want to laugh. "Go to sleep."

"I'm still going to search for Crow in the morning."

"No."

She would.

It didn't take long for Tin's heavy breaths to come out even—it seemed he could easily fall asleep at any time. A numbing tingle rippled up her left leg where Tin's side was starting to crush her. Dorothy could barely feel her limb and couldn't stay like this all night, so she tried to adjust her position while maneuvering her right leg a bit.

All that did was press her lower half to Tin. She stilled when she felt *him* against her—something hard. Tin's breaths were still even. But as she twisted a little more to drag her leg out, Tin's body froze, his breaths no longer steady.

"Sorry, that was my fault," she said, embarrassed. "I couldn't get comfortable."

"You keep making things more complicated, don't you?" He sighed. "Just. Hold on. I'm going to roll over but, for once, listen, and stay still the rest of the night." Releasing his grip on her, he carefully rolled over while she stayed on her side, planted to the dirt. The cloak continued to keep them hidden. Tin's back was now to her chest with his legs pulled up like an infant's. He wrapped one of her legs around to his stomach while the other was tucked directly under his buttocks.

"There," he muttered and went straight back to sleep.

She closed her eyes, noticing Tin's breaths didn't sound even—they were almost ragged, as though he were thinking about something else. Steadily, she brought her fingertips to his cheek where the ridges lay, and lightly brushed them across, hoping to ease him into sleep. The heat from the iron tingled and nipped at her digits. He inhaled a sharp breath, but didn't say a word. Not even his favorite word of the day—*no*.

Lowering her palm, Dorothy cradled the spot on his chest, where his stone heart rested, and remembered the young fae he'd once been. She couldn't help but imagine what his skin, beneath his shirt, would feel like against her fingertips.

Stop it, Dorothy. You're at the edge of a forest with monstrous beasts who could be watching your every move, and all you can think about is

47

touching someone's skin? Someone who has been nothing but intolerable? But she understood why he was the way he was.

The stirring of wings rumbled again—she couldn't control her body from trembling a bit as she pressed her face into Tin's warm neck. Even if she'd still had her rifle, there wouldn't have been enough bullets to slaughter them all.

CHAPTER SEVEN

TIN

If one night with Dorothy pressed against Tin wasn't enough to drive him mad, the second was. Damn whoever'd cursed those pixies who forced Tin and Dorothy beneath his cloak. *Flying monkeys*, Dorothy had called them. No doubt it was another term she'd learned from Glinda. Why Dorothy wanted to journey to that dimwitted witch was beyond him. Crow was different—they had traveled through Oz together—but Glinda hadn't done much outside of giving Dorothy the silver slippers. She had probably floated away in her fucking bubble and got distracted by will-o-wisps on her way home. She should be defending the South more, instead of letting Langwidere attempt to conquer it. Tin had kept silent on Langwidere having the western territory because he hadn't wanted to bring her name up.

"Please tell me that's a town." Dorothy hurried to Tin's side, slightly out of breath and pointing through the trees where the edge of a large village peeked through. They'd seen nothing but foliage all day so he couldn't blame her sudden burst of excitement. Their tense, silent journey was almost over for

49

another day. "It's not a trick, is it?"

The sight of thatched roofs and old, worn buildings was far from welcome. Towns meant fae. Fae meant a hassle. But the yellow brick road ran straight down the center of it. Tin had traveled across most of Oz over the years, but he'd never been to Langwidere's place before. Even if he had, he needed the brick road to navigate the South in general and they weren't too far from the border.

"It's a town," Tin grumbled.

They just weren't stepping foot in it. They needed the road, but that was easy enough to find again if they walked around this little pocket of civilization. If they kept moving, they could be in the South by nightfall. A quick break at the southern border if Dorothy needed it, and they would arrive at Langwidere's a day ahead of schedule. Resting in town would get them there on the last day of Lion's deadline, and he *wasn't* taking an entire night to rest. Dorothy, on the other hand, stumbled with each step and appeared ready to blow over with the slightest breeze.

"I can't wait to take a bath and eat something other than nuts." She let her head fall back and closed her eyes.

Tin bit his tongue to keep from reminding her that he'd hunted for their lunch hours ago. The meat was tough and clung to the bone, but it was filling enough. He hadn't *needed* to kill a second bird for her.

"And sleep in a bed ... *alone.*"

The last addition to her list set Tin on edge. It wasn't *that* bad sleeping against him, was it? He'd kept his hands to himself. Though there'd been no stopping his very obvious attraction to her when the softest part of her had been pressed against him. He *knew* she'd felt his erection last night, but his cloak wasn't big enough for them to sleep safely apart. The enchanted fabric saved them from the monstrous pixies and his body heat kept her from freezing when the temperatures had dropped. As much as he hated to admit it, Tin's hardened heart had felt something when she hadn't flinched away. Her fingers had traced his scar without any sign of disgust and her hand had rested on his chest as if it were the most natural thing in the world. Even the whores that took his coin hadn't touched him that warmly—they hadn't even *looked* at his face. But Dorothy… Her heat, her compassion, sent humming vibrations through him even now.

"We aren't staying," he said before he could stop himself.

Dorothy glared at him. "Excuse me?"

"We're continuing south."

"I told you, I'm going to find Crow. I only stayed with you another day because you promised we would find a town, and I need supplies." He should have known she hadn't let go of searching for Crow.

Tin snorted. Even with supplies, she wouldn't last a day on the yellow brick road without him. The Emerald City was even more hazardous with the continued fighting. Why Dorothy assumed Crow would still be there was beyond him. Whatever condition Crow's brain was in now, he had to be smart enough not to get involved in that power struggle.

"We did find a town." He motioned to the sleepy village. Smoke rose from chimneys, but the streets were empty as the fae settled into their homes for the evening. The rich scent of roasting meat filled the air, even this far away. It would be a lie to say it didn't make Tin's mouth water, though he knew it wasn't worth the trouble. "And now we walk around it."

Dorothy pursed her lips, a defiant gleam in her eyes, and sprinted toward the buildings.

Tin stood immobile. Never had he met someone so insolent… No one had been this utterly unafraid of his wrath in years.

Dorothy was nearly at the edge of town when he bolted after her. He snatched her wrist and spun her to his chest. A small gasp escaped her as he pressed her into a wide tree trunk, trapping her there with his weight. "No sane fae goes to the Emerald City."

"I'm not a fae, and I've been called insane on numerous

occasions," Dorothy said, her eyes becoming glassy. "If your heart is stone again, maybe Crow's brain isn't intact either. He could still be there."

Tin cursed under his breath. "Even before he got his brain unscrambled, Crow wasn't *that* stupid, so behave. You're not leaving my side until we get to Lion."

She shoved at his chest, but he didn't budge against the feeble attempt. "I'm not your prisoner, Tin. You can't force me to stay with you."

"I was paid to do a job, and I always follow through."

"Is that all I am to you?" Dorothy lifted her chin, her eyes no longer glassy. "A job?"

Was it? A muscle ticked in his jaw. She was a job but was that *all*? Dorothy wasn't like anyone else he knew—she'd grown into a fearless, determined woman. She was naïve, compassionate, bold… His gaze fell to her mouth and he leaned in. Another inch and he would be kissing her. How he wanted to close that gap. To see what she tasted like. He suppressed a groan at the thought.

She *was* a job. Soon her face—this flawless face—would no longer belong to Dorothy. It would sit in a glass case or, worse, on Langwidere's shoulders. Would Lion be with his lover while she looked like Dorothy? Would he part her lips with his tongue and explore? Stare into these warm brown eyes as he entered her? An intense wave of anger washed over Tin and he leaned in, running his nose along the soft skin of her neck.

"What are you doing?" Dorothy whispered, but didn't try to shove him away again.

What was he doing? What *the fuck* was he doing? He lifted his head just enough to meet her eyes. "We'll stay until tomorrow morning."

If they missed Lion's deadline, he wouldn't get paid, and then leading Dorothy to her death would be pointless. He could send her back to Kansas instead… Or keep her for himself… He pushed away from Dorothy, as well as his thoughts, and rubbed

52

a hand over the smooth side of his face.

"Good. You need some sleep to get rid of this attitude." Dorothy made a show of brushing off her dirty, stained clothes and stepped away from the tree.

"Dorothy?" he croaked.

She paused and looked over her shoulder at him, waiting.

"I… Townsfolk don't usually welcome me with open arms," he admitted. A small sense of shame rose inside him. The emotion startled him almost as much as the trepidation he felt at being run out of town in front of her. He didn't care about the townsfolk or their opinions. *He didn't.* Dorothy was … different.

She backtracked to him and wove her fingers between his, squeezing. "You're not the monster you think you are."

Wasn't that a nice notion? That he somehow deserved to have her holding his hand as if he hadn't used it to kill countless fae? The warmth of her skin crept through his gloves, making him want to squeeze her hand in return, but the blood of his prey had heated his hand too. Tin swallowed hard. "I'm every bit the monster and they know it."

She opened her mouth, likely to deny it again, but Tin freed his hand from hers and strode into town. All the way, he flexed his hand as he walked, still feeling her warm fingers entwined with his. The town was another full of dwarves, as most in the East were, but being closer to the southern border attracted different fae, too. Brownies, gnomes, pixies of the non-cursed variety, and even a few banshees were known in these parts. He knew because he'd been hired to kill at least one of each.

They headed down a handful of paths before seeing another soul. Tin quickly turned the marred side of his face away from the female nymph and folded his hands behind his back to hide his iron-tipped gloves. For whatever reason, he didn't want Dorothy to witness the female running away screaming.

"Hello!" Dorothy called cheerfully and waved to the nymph.

Tin sighed inwardly. *What the hell is she doing now?*

The female blinked her large green eyes in surprise. She wore a bright yellow dress made of spider silk with matching ribbons woven through her black hair and cheaply made jewelry draped around her neck. A prostitute, given her rumpled state and how her hand rested on the door to the brothel.

"Don't draw attention," Tin whispered.

Dorothy ignored the warning and approached with her hand out. "It's nice to see a friendly face."

The girl sized Dorothy up, looking strangely at her hand, as fae didn't shake, and then scanned Tin. He watched her ring-laden fingers skim down the front of her dress and tensed. If she went for a weapon, she'd be dead before she drew another breath and they'd be on their way to Lion.

"Thirty silver for both of you," she said in a sultry voice.

"For both of us?" Dorothy asked.

"Thirty silver?" Tin quickly flung his arm around Dorothy's shoulders. If she didn't want to do what she was told, he'd teach her a lesson. "That seems a bit steep."

The nymph parted her ruby lips. "It would be for you alone, but not many fae here will take a human to bed. Or rather, none of the clean ones will anyway."

Dorothy tried to jump away from Tin, but he held her to his side, without letting the iron on his face be seen. *Oh, yes,* he thought. Judging by the red creeping into her face, this was going to be more fun than he'd anticipated.

"There's been a misunderstanding," Dorothy squeaked.

"Darling, it's okay," he said in a soothing voice. "We can have fun on our own."

"We won't be doing any such thing!"

"It's disappointing, I know." He sighed loudly enough for the nymph to hear. Then Tin chuckled into Dorothy's hair and led her away from the brothel before they created a scene. "You promised to listen," he mumbled in her ear.

"All I did was say hello. There was no reason for you to..."

Tin grinned at her deepening blush. "To what?"

"Look. There's an inn," she blurted instead of answering.

She was right. An inn sat at the crossroads, but not the kind where she would want to stay. Definitely the only kind that would accept his coin, however. He let go of her and fished his money out as she hurried across the brick street. The excitement in her expression only made him worry more about the innkeeper chasing him out of town. He stretched his jaw, feeling the iron pull against his skin. An actual bed would do them both some good—after a night in the dirt—though she would need to sleep beside him again. There was no chance he was letting Dorothy have her own room when she was so adamant about going their separate ways to look for Crow.

Dorothy barely waited for him to catch up before she pushed her way through the door with another pleasant *hello*. Tin eased in after her, allowing her to steal the attention from him. Maybe he should have given her the coin to secure a room on their behalf—the innkeeper would have rented to her just to make her stop acting as if they were lifelong friends.

A beady-eyed brownie sat on a worn velvet chair with a guest book before her. Wrinkles covered her dark face and the skin on her hands was so tight it looked as if it was about to burst. She wore a high-necked black dress covered in some sort of animal fur and too much brown powder to cover her graying hair.

The brownie licked her fingertip and turned the page, pen in hand. "One room or two?"

"One," Tin said at the same time Dorothy said, "two".

The brownie paused and Tin felt her gaze sink into him. He kept his face tilted again and arranged his cloak to hide the axe at his hip. Curse his notoriety. "The Tin Man," the brownie finally squeaked, yellow eyes bulging with fear. "Not in here. No, no, no. Even I have my limits!"

Tin released a breath and faced her fully. "My companion needs to rest."

"The Knoll House has plenty of rooms available."

"But we aren't *at* the Knoll House," Tin said through his teeth. For Dorothy's sake, he tried to remain calm. He wasn't sure how long he could keep it up because he, too, had limits.

"He won't hurt anyone," Dorothy promised. He wished she hadn't. "We have enough money."

How would she know how much he carried? And how stupid of her to announce it in a place that catered to criminals and cutthroats. If someone tried to rob them, there went his promise of no killing. Tin cleared his throat.

Dorothy shot him a stern look. "Don't even try to deny it. We're staying here."

The brownie shut her book and inched closer to Dorothy. "Dearest human." She eyed Tin warily and shifted to use Dorothy's leg as a shield for her short, plump body. "Do you not know who you travel with?"

"Of course I know him."

The brownie blanched. "I can't allow it. I'll have no customers left."

Tin huffed and snatched one of the keys hanging on the wall. With a quick glance at the tag, he informed her, "We'll be in room eleven. Send food up—*no faerie fruit*. Knock and leave it outside the door."

"You can't do that!" The brownie cowered as she spoke. "Give it back!"

"You won't even know we're here," Dorothy vowed with a pleading smile.

"Leave her. She won't give us any trouble," Tin said, moving away from the frightened fae. Once again, he had to bend to keep from hitting his head as he climbed the stairs. Next time he splurged on an inn, it would be one built for someone of his height. The rooms were clearly marked with large gouges in the wooden doors, and Tin wasted no time locking them both inside theirs.

A lumpy mattress and round wooden tub took up most of the room, leaving only enough space for a one-person table and another two people to stand. It smelled awful, like mildew, wet dirt, and sex, but at least the bedding appeared fresh.

56

"You couldn't have grabbed two keys?" Dorothy cocked her head, then took in the room.

"Sorry, *princess*. Do the accommodations not suit you? We could continue on like I wanted—the brownie would be thrilled."

"I'm not continuing on with you," she said. "I'm just staying the one night and then getting supplies so I can find Crow."

"Good luck with that." Tin stuck the key in his pocket with purpose, noticing Dorothy's eyes glued to the metal. "Remember how things ended last time."

She flopped down on the bed and stretched. "I won't argue with you."

Neither would he, but he let the subject drop. She wouldn't be going anywhere. With a sigh, he sat, using the table as a chair. His fingers moved unconsciously to his face. If it wasn't for the iron snaking across his cheek, maybe he would have been able to blend in enough to secure a better room for her. A woman on the path to death deserved that much—at least *this* woman did.

"Tin, it's not so bad," Dorothy whispered. "The marks—I know you worry about them, even if you don't want to admit it. They make you look almost fierce, a beautiful sort of untamed." She cleared her throat, her face turning red. "Anyway, my point is, there's nothing wrong with them."

He snorted. "Nothing except making me look like a fierce, untamed beast, you mean."

"No. I meant that as a compliment."

Tin moved his hand to the small pieces of bone holding his hair away from his face. Maybe he should remove them. His hair would cover the worst of it. "It's not a compliment."

"You don't seem like the type to care about what other people think." She propped herself up on her elbows. "You certainly don't care what *I* think, and we were friends."

"You're right. I *don't* care," he lied. "Hiding my face just might make getting you to Lion easier on us both. Quicker money, less hassle."

She rolled her eyes and fell back onto the bed. "If believing that makes you feel better…"

The brownie left them cold stew and stale bread for a late dinner like he'd instructed, but despite the innkeeper's passive aggressive meal choices, it was the best food they'd had in days. Dorothy ate it slowly, like she was savoring each taste. Tin watched her mouth and wondered what her lips would feel like on his. On his neck, his stomach. Lower.

Right at dusk, Dorothy fell into a blissful sleep, unaware of his thoughts. But time passed and Tin couldn't make the lewd ideas disappear. How would her hair feel if he buried his fingers into it? What sounds would she make? He grazed her cheek with his knuckles as she slumbered. Even with his gloves on, it sent a thrill through him. His balls ached from denying his release day after day and he shifted uncomfortably. The problem could be solved rather quickly if he wasn't afraid Dorothy would wake up to the sight of him stroking himself. *Ah, hell.* He shouldn't have even let the thought surface because now his cock was rising to the occasion.

The thin blanket did nothing to hide Dorothy's curves. Beneath her clothes, he wondered what her naked body looked like, how heavy her breasts would feel in his hands, how her legs would feel wrapped around his waist as he thrust inside her. A sweat broke on the back of his neck.

The brothel.

It was right across the street and Dorothy was fast asleep. The innkeeper wouldn't come knocking if she didn't see Tin leave so Dorothy would be safe here alone. He could be quick about it. Who was he kidding? It *would* be quick after suffering temptation for so long.

That settled it.

Tin carefully got up from the edge of the bed, slipped from

the room, and locked Dorothy in again without making a sound. He used his cloak to move through the hallway and lobby unseen and entered the brothel across the street without drawing any attention.

Half-naked fae worked the opulent room, leaning over males as they played cards and perching on their laps in the sitting area. Pillows were strewn on couches and in corners. A deep purple rug padded the center of a gleaming crystal floor. Faerie lights floated near the ceiling, casting a soft glow down onto the room and its inhabitants. Wall murals depicted a variety of sexual scenes, some subtle, others perverse, in deep, sensual colors. The artist was so skilled that it looked to Tin as if he could feel the faes' satiny skin if he grazed the wall.

The workers were a menu of endless variety. If one preferred horns or wings or pointed teeth, they could be found under this roof, but Tin wasn't picky. He couldn't afford to be. The gems of any brothel, however, were the nymphs, because they actually enjoyed the profession. Each of the nymphs in this establishment wore a different jewel colored gown with stone or ribbons in their hair and the perfect blend of color painted on their delicate faces. Tin's breath grew ragged knowing one of them would be beneath him soon.

"Can I help you, my lord?" a female asked. Tin turned to see the nymph in the yellow dress from earlier. She was put together now, hair brushed to a shine and dress smoothed of its wrinkles. "Oh, it's you. Where's your human friend?"

Tin suppressed a snarl. "Forget you saw her."

She ran a hand down his arm, making his cock grow even harder as he thought about Dorothy stroking his skin instead. *Damn it.* Why did she have to bring Dorothy up? She was the last person he wanted to think about right now.

"In that case, what's your pleasure?" the female asked.

A nymph in a blue dress caught his eye on the other side of the room. Wavy brown hair fell to her hips with strands of pearls worked into a circlet of braids. Deep brown eyes met his. He adjusted his pants as he stepped away from the female in yellow. "She is."

Tin tried not to think about how much she resembled Dorothy as he approached. He would need to pay her an exorbitant amount to have him, he knew, but he would gladly do so.

"Good evening, my lord," she said in a sweet voice. "Are you here for a game of cards?"

Tin didn't even spare a look at the gaming table beside her. "I'm here for company."

"Wonderful." Her smile was only slightly believable as she scanned him up and down. He knew he appeared unnerving—partially hidden beneath a cloak—but he didn't care. As long as she didn't scream when she saw his face without the hood, recognizing him as the Tin Man. "Follow me upstairs, won't you?"

Moans of other patrons' pleasure, mixed with the creaking of beds, filled the second floor. Incense floated through the air and Tin nearly moaned himself. It was no surprise the brothel was infused with the scent of an aphrodisiac. They wanted customers in and out to make more money. Tin had nearly been mad with need before, but now, he was worried about making it to the room without taking the nymph against the wall right there in the hallway.

"After you, my lord," the female in blue said and held back a thick red curtain to her room. A large bed covered in silks and furs waited inside but the room was otherwise empty.

He took one step toward the room and froze when he heard his name from the room next door.

"The Tin Man, yes," said a male. The curtain was closed so he couldn't see who the voice belonged to. "Have you seen him?"

"I think I would remember a beast like that," the female replied.

"And the human girl? Brown hair, about this tall…"

"Forgive me, my lord, but we don't see many humans in these parts. Are you sure I can't—"

A hand touched Tin's and he jerked back to find the nymph staring at him. "Is everything all right?" she asked.

Shit. Shit, shit, shit.

His cock throbbed painfully, but if someone had tracked them here, Dorothy could be in danger. And he'd left her alone for *this*.

"No need," the mystery male said. "If you do see them, please leave word for Crow with your madam and I'll check back before I head south."

Crow.

No. It couldn't be him. What would he be doing here? And why? There was no reason he should even know Dorothy had returned to Oz. If Dorothy found out he was looking for her, Tin would have to drag her to Lion unconscious. And Crow… If he discovered why Tin was taking Dorothy south, Crow would do everything in his power to stop him.

Shit!

Tin turned on his heel and bolted back to the inn. He'd never moved so fast in his life. Everything and everyone in his peripheral vision became a blur, while his rapid breath echoed in his ears.

The door to his inn room was suddenly in front of him, the key in his fingertips. He fumbled to fit it into the lock with shaking hands. On the third attempt, it slid in and Tin shoved his way inside to find Dorothy exactly where he'd left her. Breath filled his tight, burning lungs. Every muscle relaxed at once and he leaned against the door, sliding to the floor.

It wasn't until he wiped the sweat from his forehead that he realized he was worried—not because he wanted Lion's money, but because he wasn't ready to *not* see her again. Whatever that meant. If the bed had been empty, he wasn't sure what his reaction would've been.

But she *was* there. Her lips were parted, her chest rising and falling with each steady breath. He wanted to touch her flawless skin like she had touched his iron mark, to give her the same warm feeling her touch had given to him.

Tin gripped the fabric over his chest. Something behind his breastbone cracked, shattered, exploded and a painful pounding suddenly assaulted him from the inside out. He gasped, his wide gaze locking onto Dorothy's sleeping form. The raging pulse in his ears, the heavy *thump thump thump* beneath his ribs. His heart. It was back.

Fuck!

CHAPTER EIGHT

DOROTHY

The heavy thud of booted footsteps against the wooden floor drew Dorothy out from her dreamless sleep. Her eyes flicked open, but she didn't move as Tin reentered the inn bedroom. His body slumped to the floor. Where had he gone? Had he left her here to go and get inebriated? She hadn't even heard him leave. It must have been the journey, making her more exhausted than usual, even though her endurance was typically steady because of the farm work.

What is he doing? Dorothy thought as he stood back up and came her way.

As Tin crept closer to the bed, slower than usual, Dorothy kept her breathing even, in and out, out and in, because she had a plan. She was no longer tired, but wide awake.

She and Tin weren't near the flying monkey beasts who howled through the night. There were only the sounds of the normal night world—bugs chirping. Beside her, the mattress dipped, slightly shaking her body. Tin seemed to hesitate before lying beside her, close, smelling of incense, his warmth practically cocooning her. It was that same feeling as when his body had been pressed against her at that tree, his nose brushing her neck, the feel of *him* against her the other night. And even then, he'd been mostly insufferable. But...

Steady. Keep breathing steady. Tin was once her friend, even if he believed he wasn't now, he could be again—once she cracked open his stone heart. His arm slipped around her, almost hesitantly, but she knew it was most likely so she wouldn't try and run off. After what seemed like forever, finally, Tin's breaths came slow and even.

Dorothy gave it a few extra moments before, ever so slowly, she rolled to face him. Even in the dark, she wasn't afraid of him, whether he wielded an axe or not. What she wondered was how anyone could ever be afraid of his soulful face.

She'd read such macabre books as *The Phantom of the Opera, Grimms' Fairy Tales, Dr. Jekyll and Mr. Hyde,* and the creatures in those books were ones to be feared, not Tin, not his face.

Staying silent as snowflakes falling in winter, Dorothy once again shifted her hand toward Tin's pocket of his pants. He'd woken the last time she'd done this at the previous inn—this time she'd be more careful. Her movements remained quiet, feather-light, like a true pickpocket as she pressed her fingers inside the place where the key to her escape lay hidden. An unexpected image came to her then, one of her slipping her hand elsewhere, into the waistband of Tin's pants. She froze as certain parts of her tingled at the thought—she hurried and pushed it away. *How un-lady-like, Dorothy.* It wasn't as if she was a virginal woman anyway—she'd lain with Jimmy before.

Holding her breath and a shiver back at the same time, Dorothy pushed her fingers farther in, then felt the brass against her digits. With caution, she dragged the key out, inch by daunting inch. Until it was fully in her grasp.

Dorothy couldn't help but grin, yet the tricky part would be getting out of the bed and then the room. She rolled over and scooted to the edge of the mattress before placing her shoes on.

Tightening her grip on the key, she tiptoed her way across the wood floor to the door. The room was too dark to see clearly, and she strained her eyes as she lifted the key to press into the lock. When she turned the key to the right, there was a soft click. She stilled before glancing over her shoulder, prepared for Tin to rip away the key and hold her in his arms once more. He didn't—he still lay in bed, fast asleep.

Turning the knob, Dorothy took a step out into the dimly-lit hallway and locked the door behind her with the key. She tossed the brass key into the air and caught it with a smile on her face. *Now who is the one locked in the room? Not me, that's who.*

She wished she could see Tin's face when he woke to discover he'd been outwitted. With quick footsteps, Dorothy hurried down the stairs to the front desk, passing a brownie who was paying no mind to her as he wrote on a sheet of paper with a quill. He grunted as she bid him a goodbye, still keeping his nose buried in whatever he was writing.

The Emerald City had become a place that was no longer alluring. Battle for control raged inside, and she knew she couldn't go in there with only a measly knife. She should have also taken Tin's axe for this little bit of her journey—too late for that. Tin had warned her that the night wasn't safe, but it wasn't a haven the last time she was here either.

Where could she find something better to use? Then Dorothy remembered the nymph in the yellow dress at the brothel that she and Tin had run into earlier. Perhaps the nymph would help her, but there might be a price. Dorothy was sure she could barter something. If not, maybe the nymph could at least point her in another direction.

She rushed across the yellow brick road and through tufts of grass toward the brothel. The grimy windows of the building were lit by dozens and dozens of candles, and the thatched roof appeared as though it might cave in at any moment.

As she opened the door and walked inside, the air struck her nose, reeking of sex, ale, and perfume. To her left rested a cluster of tables filled with patrons, touching their hired fae for the night while playing cards. At a table in the corner, a fae sat with flowing blonde hair and goat horns sprouting from her forehead, while a male with his shirt unbuttoned painted her. Against the opposite wall stood another couple—a faerie with long lilac wings draping the floor as her hands ran up her client's chest. Dorothy didn't want to watch all of this, but she couldn't fight the allure of it all. She finally tore her gaze away and took a step forward when an arm dropped down around her shoulders.

"Hello, beautiful, I think I've been bewitched," a voice slurred at her ear. "I didn't know mortals worked in this part of Oz."

Dorothy could barely move as her eyes met a fae male with sleek black hair, eyes the color of tree bark, faun ears, and curving horns. "I'm sorry, I won't be here long."

"It would only take a moment to slip inside you, and I've never been in a mortal before. I'll pay whatever you wish," he purred at her ear as her eyes widened in surprise.

Before she could say no and move away, a voice spoke up from behind her, "She doesn't work here. Now drop your arm from her, because she's mine."

"Sorry, Falyn," the faun said in a sullen voice, "I didn't realize she was already taken." He pried his arm from Dorothy's shoulders, turned on his hoofed feet, and headed to a velvet settee where a group of nymphs wearing see-through scarves were feeding each other green faerie fruit.

Dorothy focused on the fae she'd been looking for, still wearing her canary-yellow dress made of spider silk and matching ribbon in her obsidian hair. The nymph—Falyn—wrapped her hand around Dorothy's wrist and tugged her to the very back of the room, to two high-backed chairs in a darkened corner.

Falyn pushed Dorothy into one of the chairs and hovered over her. The nymph's moss-colored eyes open wide. "What's your name?" Her words came out in a rush.

Dorothy's brows lowered in confusion. She'd come here to find Falyn and now it seemed as though the nymph had been looking for her. "Why?"

"Just, what is it?"

Tin would have told her to be quiet and not answer, but he wasn't there, and she wasn't going to listen to anyone except herself. Besides, Dorothy believed that Falyn might be willing to help after ridding her of the faun. "Dorothy."

Lips parting, the nymph's hand flew to her mouth and her green eyes lit up with glee. "As in Dorothy Gale? It is, isn't it? He's looking for you."

Dorothy stilled, scanning the room, prepared to find Tin already there with his axe in hand. But he wasn't anywhere in sight. "What do you mean exactly? Who?"

"Crow," Falyn whispered. "He was here earlier, asking about you. I didn't know he was here, but Chara came and told me Crow had come, sniffing around for the Tin Man and a human woman. Chara hadn't seen you two, but then it clicked that I had."

Dorothy perked up, leaning forward while growing anxious. "I need to find him. That's actually why I came back here, because I was going to see about getting supplies to retrieve him from the Emerald City. Where is he?" She searched the room, not seeing a single sign of him. Perhaps he was in one of the other rooms.

"He already left." Falyn shrugged. "But he did mention something to Chara about heading south."

Dorothy stood from her chair. "I'd better hurry so I can get to him." The sooner she left, the sooner she could catch up and find him.

Falyn placed a hand on Dorothy's shoulder. "You may not be heading to the Emerald City any longer, but you can't go empty-handed, either. The South is dangerous, too."

"I don't have any money." She patted the pockets of her overalls, knowing nothing but lint rested inside. "Perhaps I could barter by bringing you back something?"

"You're Dorothy Gale." Falyn smiled. "You destroyed the Wicked Witch of the West, and even with our world in shambles at the moment, I believe now that you're back, all can be righted once again."

What the fae of Oz didn't realize was that Dorothy had always been just a girl. It was all because of the silver slippers—that was what had given her the magic to defeat the Wicked Witch. And anyone who put on those slippers could have done the same, but for some reason no one seemed to care about that fact. She thought back to when she'd reentered Oz and there had been a statue built of her. If she did get the slippers again, maybe she could help like she had before.

"Follow me," Falyn continued and waved her down a narrow hallway with walls covered in gold leaves and copper branches. Dorothy could only focus on the moans and groans coming from behind the closed curtains.

Falyn opened the curtain to a room smelling of rose petals, with only a bed, a vanity, and a wardrobe. From beneath the bed, Falyn pulled out a sheathed machete. She handed it, along with the strap, to Dorothy. "You can wear it."

"Are you sure?" Dorothy asked, tightening it on her back. She was used to a rifle, but this would be perfect. No bullets to run out of.

"Yes."

She peered up at Falyn and slid the knife from her pocket. "I know it's not an even trade, but keep this."

Falyn rolled the small blade in her hand. "I like this better. No one will see it coming if I need to use it."

Dorothy hoped Falyn wouldn't have to use it. "If Tin comes, please don't tell him I was here."

"He was actually here not too long ago," Falyn said, studying her with what might have been sympathy.

"He was?" But then she recognized the smell of incense, the one that had come from Tin when he'd slipped into bed.

"Yes." She nodded. "He went to see one of the other nymphs."

Tin hadn't been drunk off of wine—he'd been delirious from sex, or perhaps both. "Oh." Dorothy couldn't stop to wonder about why it felt like a punch to the chest. She also couldn't help but imagine what it would be like to have Tin's naked body, slick with sweat, moving against hers while her unclothed form was heated head to toe from his touch.

Dorothy shook away the thought. She needed to make herself focus only on getting to Crow. Now that she knew she wouldn't have to fight her way through the Emerald City to find him, it would hopefully make things much easier. "Thank you, Falyn."

"Never thank a fae." Falyn shot her a glare. "But in this case, you're welcome. Be sure to keep your head on your shoulders. Even with Glinda there, the South isn't a good place to be anymore. Most have fled."

The East hadn't been too terribly bad. How much worse could the South be? "Tin told me it's not like it used to be."

Falyn nodded and looked like she wanted to say more, but Dorothy needed to leave.

With a goodbye, Dorothy headed out of the brothel and back into the starry night. She stepped onto the yellow brick road, feeling every crack and broken piece beneath her feet.

While she should be shifting all her attention to Crow, Dorothy could only think about Tin entwined with another female. An anger came then, one she didn't understand, but she let that emotion fuel her as she took off at a fast sprint. There was no time to dally and walk when she could reach Crow much quicker if she just ran. Together, they would get to Glinda. But a fear nagged at her... What if Crow was changed like Tin?

CHAPTER NINE

TIN

*Th*ump-thump. *Thump-thump.*

The pace of Tin's now-beating heart tugged him slowly from a deep sleep. His chest was raw and vulnerable over the unfamiliar organ. He hadn't expected to regain a real heart— hadn't *wanted* to—but he felt more alive than ever now. It returned to stone so long ago that he forgot how the steady rhythm flowed from head-to-toe.

Tin thought once his heart was encased in stone again, it would remain that way. That the Wizard had pulled a horrible trick on him. The strength of his pulse had lessened so subtly over the first two years with the beating organ that he hadn't noticed he was in trouble until the day he'd woken up to find it had changed back to a solid stone in his chest, but now he knew the truth. His heart had never truly been lost to the curse. It was waiting. Waiting for Dorothy to return and break it open again. All it took was her touch, genuine and unafraid.

Tin stretched across the too-small mattress with a faint smile and cracked a few aching joints. The pillow smelled vaguely of piss, but it wasn't the worst place he'd laid his head. He was just relieved to have finally gotten a good night's rest after having had Dorothy pressed—

Holy shit.

Dorothy.

Tin jerked forward and ran his hands frantically over the empty bed as if it would somehow summon her. When it didn't, he flew to his feet and spun, hoping she was anywhere else in the tiny room. His breaths became labored. This was impossible. How? Unless that good for nothing brownie had another key and a severe death wish. He would kill everything under three feet tall until one of them produced Dorothy. *Unbelievable!* Oh, the ways he was going to punish the devious little innkeeper for this. He swept his axe up and attempted to wrench the door open. The wood shuddered but the locked door held fast. Tin growled angrily and dug into his pocket for the key.

The world seemed to still for a long moment. It was gone. The key was *gone!* He *knew* he'd locked the door before he got back in bed with Dorothy—his resurrected heart beat like a caged bird. Thinking the key fell out while he slept, Tin ripped the sheets away and shook the blankets. He knelt to look beneath the bed. Nothing. The key was nowhere to be seen.

The truth trickled in slowly. Tin wanted to deny that Dorothy could've gotten the key off him while he slept, but couldn't. The relief at seeing her in the room, not stolen away by Crow, and the shock of his heart returning, had pulled him into a deep sleep. Too deep, considering the danger lurking in every direction. The breaking of his curse seemed to have worn him out in every sense of the word. Not only had Dorothy put her hand in his pocket and extracted the key, but also climbed out from beneath his arm to get off the bed, opened the door, *and* locked it again.

"Damn it!" Tin's blood boiled at his negligence. At Dorothy's utter disregard for her own safety.

Tin gripped his axe tighter and slammed it into the door.

71

Again and again he swung. Splinters flew all around him as he demolished the wood. When it was nothing more than a frame with hinges and a knob, he stormed through the jagged hole.

Two beady-eyed brownies stared in horror as he strode down the stairs, then he impaled the axe into the record book. The young, pale-skinned female sitting at the entrance leapt back, knocking over her tall chair. Tin took two heaving breaths before regaining his ability to speak. "What have you done with her?"

The brownie squeaked unintelligibly.

It took every ounce of Tin's self-control not to kill her then and there, but he needed her answer first. Returned heart be damned. "Where. Is. The. Girl?"

"She left shortly after you returned," the bearded male yelped from the top of the staircase. "Walked right out the door, she did."

Tin straightened his back, shoulders stiff. Fucking Dorothy and her fucking determination to find Crow. And that piece of shit witch, Glinda. Dorothy *knew* Tin wouldn't let her out of his sight if she waited until morning. Knew he wouldn't allow her to find supplies and waltz off. So instead, Dorothy had decided to get herself killed because, apparently, Crow was more important than her own life.

"Was she alone?" Tin demanded.

The brownie nodded.

Of course she was. Because she was *fucking stupid*. What more proof did she need that Oz was dangerous? The yellow brick road was destroyed, the Emerald City a battle ground, and cursed pixies trolled the land every night. If anything harmed her, it would be her own fault. Not that he wouldn't track and kill whatever dared touch her.

Hypocrite, Tin chided himself. Hadn't he originally been leading Dorothy to two fae who would commit the worst kind of violence against her? Maybe Dorothy wasn't so stupid after all. Maybe she *should* be running away from him. It didn't hurt any less that she'd fled in the middle of the night. *Damn his heart*

72

for coming back now. This would be so much easier if he didn't have feelings to contend with.

Tin tore through the front door of the inn and froze. Where would she have gone? Back toward the Emerald City? Even though he told her there was no way Crow was still there...

Fuck.

He covered his face with his free hand, ignoring the burn from the iron tipped glove, and tried to piece together what Dorothy might do. She wasn't a little girl anymore and he'd only known *this* Dorothy for a few days. He didn't know how she thought. Fae were easier to read, easier to predict. Money and power fueled them while something else fueled Dorothy.

Money and power.

The brothel. Crow had told the nymph he would be back to check with the madam before he left town. If he hadn't returned, that meant he was still nearby. Unless he didn't have to check because he found someone else who'd seen Dorothy...

Tin shook the thought from his mind and raced back to the brothel. The door slammed against the inner wall, startling dazed patrons and workers alike. The madam could've been any of them or none of them, but Crow, Tin knew, wouldn't go unnoticed.

"Did Crow come back?" he boomed, drawing every eye in the room.

The fae shifted, filling the air with tension, as Tin's identity finally broke through their drugged haze. A lanky elf shoved a naked, horned female from her lap and screamed. Pandemonium followed. Chairs fell as their occupants scrambled to their feet— a smaller fae tripped over the displaced furniture, before a hoofed creature trampled it. Males shoved their prostitutes in Tin's direction and raced for the back exit. The females cried. One fainted. It was an overly-dramatic scene that Tin didn't want to deal with.

"Damn useless pieces of shit!" he roared.

There would be no answers here. He turned on his heel and

73

tried to remember what he knew of Crow from before, when the fae's brain had still been a mess. A loner. Quiet. Enjoyed working with his hands. But then he got his brain fixed and damned if Tin knew what his personality was like now.

Think, Tin, think.

Crow wouldn't want to stay in town, even one as quiet as this. He preferred nature to an actual shelter, and that much couldn't have changed. To the woods, then. Somewhere close, but not too close... Tin grumbled a string of curses and set off for the edge of town.

Two perimeter sweeps of the woods later, one farther out from town than the first, Tin finally came across his first clue to Crow's whereabouts. An elvish song carried through the trees, deep and gentle. Tin scanned the branches above in search of the cursed pixies and found them blissfully empty. Only Crow would be stupid enough to camp in these woods and purposely draw attention to himself.

Tin's heart thundered in his chest as he tracked the somber song through the woods. He shoved down all traces of emotion that tried to barrel into his thoughts. Dorothy was about to regret running. Almost as much as Crow was about to regret luring her to a place as dangerous as these woods. If Dorothy had told Crow they were heading to Lion, they would both regret it because then Tin would have to fight for Dorothy. When Tin fought, he won, and he didn't particularly want to slaughter Crow. At least not in front of Dorothy, when she clearly cared for him. But why should he care how Dorothy felt? She clearly didn't care how *he* felt. Even if she did care, Crow was nothing but a nuisance to Tin. So what if Dorothy hated him for the last day or two of her life? He'd leave her to Langwidere and walk away a richer fae. His heart would harden again soon enough if history was any indication, and any reservations he had would

74

die along with it.

The thought soured his stomach. *No*. Whatever Dorothy did, however she hurt him, he wouldn't give her to Lion or Langwidere. Any thought of doing so now was as silent as his chest had been yesterday morning.

The trees thinned and Tin paused. This was where the song originated, but there was no Crow. He stared at the dead leaves scattered over exposed dirt and listened harder as his hand drifted to the head of his axe. The song ended abruptly and Tin ground his teeth together in annoyance.

"You could simply ask me to come down," Crow said from above. "No need to chop down any trees, Woodsman."

Tin's gaze snapped up to find a dark canvas stretched between two thick branches. Dark blue leaves camouflaged the hammock in thick foliage, the fabric swinging slightly when a pointed black boot appeared over the side. The movement sent a few brittle, dying leaves floating gently toward Tin's head.

Relief at finding Crow faded almost instantly when he remembered that it meant actually having to *deal* with Crow. Ten years apart wasn't nearly enough. Once Dorothy left, Crow did too, taking off on his own without so much as a goodbye to anyone in the Emerald City. *Selfish bastard.* "There's no need to take your name seriously either, and yet you've nested twenty feet off the ground."

"Says the fae with metal burned into his face."

Iron wasn't tin, but he had bigger things to worry about. "Get your ass down here."

There was a brief moment of silence before Crow exhaled loudly. A dark figure dropped from the hammock, landing in a crouched position, like he was a fucking bird. Crow rose slowly, straightening his spine, looking every bit like a shadow of death when he'd probably never killed a thing in his miserable life.

Dark feathers were braided into Crow's long black hair. His locks cascaded over his shoulders from beneath a sleek black mask shaped like a beak. The slope came to a point near his chin while the back flared up in an elegant curve. Thin, hand-knotted ropes draped down his bare, muscular chest in varying lengths, ending just above his belt.

"I've been looking for you," Crow admitted. He pulled the mask from his face to reveal light brown eyes, high cheek bones, and a faint horizontal scar over the bridge of his nose.

"Not just me," Tin accused. "Where's Dorothy?"

Crow's eyes widened. "Isn't she with you? Word came to me from the dwarves that you brought her back and were traveling together."

Damn dwarves. One of them must've seen him drag Dorothy through the portal. "Do you see her?" he growled, stepping forward.

Crow glanced into the woods behind Tin. "She isn't hidden somewhere safe?"

"Don't play games with me." Tin advanced on Crow and grabbed him by the throat. "She snuck out of the inn after insisting we find *you*. Do you really expect me to believe you *just happened* to be in town the same night she disappears?"

Crow stared Tin in the eye, unfazed by the violence. "If Dorothy isn't with you and she isn't with me, it seems we share a problem."

Tin released Crow and roared. He didn't care if a swarm of cursed pixies descended on him—killing them might release some of the anger and fear swirling through Tin's body. His heart was beating fast, urging him to calm down, and he wanted to rip it out and slam the bloody thing against a tree. He ignored it once more and instead slammed his axe into the nearest trunk. "Damn, stubborn woman!"

CHAPTER TEN

DOROTHY

Dorothy hadn't stopped much throughout the night, only when strange howling sounds had erupted close to the path. She'd hid behind a bush for a long while until the thumping of feet and growls took off in another direction. The road before her had then slipped into complete darkness the further she got away from the village. While she continued alone, her determination to get to the South and find Crow had left her fearless. If she'd slept or turned around, then she could have missed Crow. But she hadn't encountered him. Where was he? What if she was wasting her time coming this way?

As the sun fully plopped itself into the deep blue sky, Dorothy ate a few nuts. Her stomach wanted more than that—she yearned to taste a bright green piece of fruit from the trees just ahead, but she couldn't.

A wooden board—painted bright pink and gold was centered on tall posts, with cursive words etched in—caught her attention. *The South*. She'd made it.

Her chest sank—if Crow had already made it to the South,

he could be anywhere. Dorothy took a few steps farther, past a curve and trees with yellow-flowered branches surrounding the path. As she pushed a limb aside and stepped through, her breath caught. The architecture was so different than that of the East and the Emerald City. Beneath her feet, the yellow brick road was no longer broken. She wondered what the North and the West looked like.

All the buildings around were boxy and painted in bright hues. Some in multicolor. It was a territory fit for a queen, and couldn't have been more fitting for Glinda. Tin had mentioned that all the territories had problems, but there were no dilapidated buildings here, no sounds of battle taking place. The world was perfectly quiet.

"Take a deep breath, Dorothy. You've always started tasks alone, or mostly alone. This is just a new task." She rotated her exhausted shoulders, feeling the machete's protection snuggly against her back.

Dorothy trekked down a small hill. At its base rested several pink and purple buildings. *Po's Bakery, Saya's Meats, June's Tricks.*

Perhaps Crow stopped at one of the shops. He always loved indulging in food.

The South stayed utterly quiet as she continued forward to one of the shops. It seemed almost strange after dodging flying monkeys and seeing other villagers for days.

She gripped the doorknob, shaped like a carrot, and pulled open the entrance to June's Tricks. Inside the building rested four small tables with stools surrounding them. Cups for tea or coffee were set in each of the customers' spots, but the place sat empty. An odor assaulted her nose—something rotten.

"Hello?" Dorothy called, approaching the stone counter. Three wicker baskets rested on top with balls of yarn and knitting hooks.

No reply.

When she reached the counter, Dorothy touched a ball of pink yarn. She leaned her head over the counter and gasped.

With her hands flying up to cover her mouth, she stumbled back, knocking a basket to the floor, a ball of yarn unraveling as it rolled near a table. "No," she whispered.

It wasn't as though she'd never seen a dead body with no head attached before. Tin had cut off the head of the addict who'd attacked her on the yellow brick road. But this was different, much different.

She took the machete from her back and moved around the counter to see if she'd been mistaken. She wasn't. There was indeed no head. Only a body in a flowy pale-blue dress speckled with dried blood. A dark crimson stain covered the floor where the head should have been. The flesh had grown gray and shriveled, and she didn't want to think about how long the body had been laying here.

There was nothing Dorothy could do, so she flew out the door of the shop and hurried in to the pink building next door. No one. Her gaze drifted from the paintings of fae on the wall, to the empty yellow settees, then fell to the corner of the room. She'd been wrong—the place wasn't empty. Resting in the dark corner lay a body sprawled in an awkward position, wearing a crimson dress. The body was skeletal, with no head attached, like the one from the other shop. Dark stains were splattered on the wall and across the floor. Tin was telling the truth—Lion really needed her. Something sinister was lurking within the quiet of the South.

Dorothy was hesitant to go into the last building, but she crept slowly, gripping her machete. If someone was in there, alive, she could question them, but considering what she'd seen, she didn't hold much hope.

As soon as she opened the door to the bakery, a loud scream echoed off the walls. Dorothy straightened, meeting the stares of two fae females. One wore her hair in two ropey braids and the other had short, wild locks and an upturned nose.

"Sorry," Dorothy rushed the words out. "I didn't mean to frighten you, but I went to the other buildings…"

The two faes' eyes shifted from wooden benches to the corner of the room and Dorothy's gaze followed. And then she noticed the smell. Another body, this one laying in what once may have been a pool of crimson blood around a headless form.

Dorothy tightened her fingers around the machete, not taking her eyes off the two fae. Could they have done this? None of the bodies appeared fresh with the exception of this one. "What happened?"

The fae with the two ropey braids took a step forward. Dorothy noticed a raised pink scar running down her left cheek. "She wanted her head..."

Dorothy froze, her brows drawing together. "Who did?"

A soft whimper came. The fae with short hair stood trembling, her face also marred by a thick scar. "Langwidere. Our older sister—Natal—had sent us away, promised to meet up with us, and when she didn't come, we returned. And this is all that was left of her."

"Who's Langwidere?" Dorothy tried to recall hearing the name when she was here last, or even when she was with Tin. It wasn't familiar in the slightest.

Dorothy remembered something Falyn had said. *Be sure to keep your head on your shoulders.* She shuddered at what she now knew to be a warning.

The braided-haired fae clasped her mouth as she began to cry, tears sliding down her cheeks. "I can say no more. But me and the one sister I have left are leaving. We won't be coming back. I'll tell you now, if you stay here, with a face like that, then you're as good as dead. I suggest marring your flesh, too." With that, she grabbed the other fae's hand and scrambled out from the building, leaving Dorothy once again alone. This time, a heavy chill raced through her bones.

A loud noise came from outside and Dorothy stilled. Her fingers dug into the machete, her knuckles turning white. She didn't believe for a second that the two fae had come back, so she scurried behind the counter, peeking her head forward at the glass display case. Behind her, the scent of bread lingered in the area. The door creaked open with a loud thud and in walked a fae male.

"I can smell you," he said.

"Not a step further," Dorothy warned, rising from her position. She'd used a machete plenty of times in the corn field. Swiping one measly male fae if she had to wouldn't be a problem.

But then she caught sight of the male's cloak, with fur stitched in at the top like a lion's mane from her world. Her gaze settled on his fur-lined boots, his long blond hair, golden irises, the tail swinging behind his back.

Her eyes widened. "Lion," she whispered. On instinct, she wanted to run toward him and wrap him in a hug, but she remembered what had happened with Tin. He'd changed, seen her differently. What if it was the same with Lion?

He straightened, his face appearing almost regal, confidence wafting off him. In her world, any woman would swoon over him. His face held a certain androgynous beauty. Yet he didn't have a face like Tin. Why was she thinking about Tin's face now?

"Who are you?" he cooed, inching closer, ever the animal.

"It's me. Dorothy." She couldn't have been that unrecognizable to him too. Her *face* was the same, even if her body wasn't.

Lion's expression appeared stunned for a moment before his eyes narrowed as he searched around the small area. "Where's Tin?"

"I..." She bit her lip. "It's not his fault. I left while he slept to come here and search for Crow."

"It really is you, then?" Lion smiled. It was the same smile he'd worn when she'd found him in the forest, where she'd offered to save him and bring him with her, Crow, and Tin to the Emerald City.

He held out his arms and she rushed forward, folding herself around him. "I've missed you." She sighed, inhaling the fur scent of his cloak.

"I've missed you more, Dorothy," he said, stroking her hair.

"What is going on here?" she mumbled into his chest. "There are decapitated bodies in all the shops! I ran into two fae who wanted me to cut my face and mentioned someone named Langwidere. This fae named Langwidere has been taking heads!" She didn't cry, only held onto her friend tighter.

Lion rotated his shoulders, pulled back, and held her upper arms gently. "Let me take you to Glinda. She'll be able to explain everything."

"Glinda's all right?" Dorothy exclaimed, a new sense of hope filling her chest. Glinda had given her advice about how to defeat the Wicked Witch. She knew how to get around, be sneaky, and get things done.

"She is," Lion murmured, bowing his head, "but for how long? She needs your help, just like the last time you were here. Langwidere's tactics have gotten more savage."

"I'll go with you, but what about Crow?" Dorothy couldn't forget about him. He'd already been without a working brain once. What if this Langwidere had already taken his head after he'd gotten here? She held the nausea stirring inside her back.

"He's already there."

CHAPTER ELEVEN

TIN

Returning to town was the furthest thing from safe. For the residents—not Tin. He couldn't care less if anyone tried to flee the moment they saw him, or tried to attack him. In fact, he would welcome it. Maybe spilling a bit of blood would help calm him down so he could focus on a plan. His brain was dizzy with thoughts of where Dorothy might be, what danger could've befallen her, if she was hungry, hurt, lost…

There his heart was, kicking in again.

"Wait here," Crow said outside the brothel.

Tin jerked at the sound of his voice. Crow hadn't spoken a word since collecting his hammock, placing his mask back over his face, and telling Tin to save his energy for the cursed pixies when this was all over.

What if they'd decided to venture closer to the South to hunt Dorothy?

He felt the blood drain from his face at the thought. It wasn't rational—there was countless prey in the woods for the pixies to hunt near the capital—but it was possible. That was enough to make him worry. "We don't have time for this. How many more businesses did you ask to rat us out?"

"All of them," Crow said casually. "But if you think I hadn't heard of your late night visit to a lovely nymph, you're wrong. Go on. Applaud me for my restraint."

Tin fought the heat rising in his cheeks. He wasn't proud of what he'd almost done at the brothel. Maybe if he admitted it was Dorothy he wanted, admitted he *felt* something when he was around her, she would have accepted him. Then her ass wouldn't have run off in the middle of the night. Because it would have been rocking beneath him, her body and his both covered in sweat.

"Your restraint?" Tin mocked.

"I had half a mind to bust through your inn room door but didn't want to jeopardize Dorothy's safety."

So he knew where they were staying, yet waited. *The fool.* If he'd come after Dorothy last night, she wouldn't be lost right now and the whole situation with Crow would've already concluded. With Dorothy at his side and Crow far, far away, even if Tin had to tie him to a tree to accomplish it.

"I wouldn't hurt her," he snarled.

"No?" Crow's masked face tilted. "Why don't I believe that?"

Tin opened his mouth to argue but Crow swept into the building. The door shut in Tin's face with a quiet thunk. Did Crow really think he would've hurt Dorothy? She was infuriating, but he wouldn't have raised a hand to her. The worst he'd done was intimidate her, but she deserved that for refusing to listen. It was her safety at risk when she ignored him. *Shit.* Why was he wasting time worrying about her safety instead of worrying about his bounty? Her head was practically in one of Langwidere's infamous glass cases already because *he'd* brought her through the portal, because *he'd* dragged her south. Getting paid was the least he could expect, but he would rather keep Dorothy. He would rather *save* Dorothy, even if it meant losing her to the mortal world again.

Fuck. His. Heart.

"She went south," Crow said as he emerged again, chest heaving.

Tin rubbed his chest where his heart throbbed painfully. "Are you sure? Is your source reliable?"

"Don't worry your pretty face. I want to find Dorothy as much as you do. She and I have too much to discuss for us to follow false leads."

Any lead could be false. Tin had followed many when tracking his targets and that was when things usually ended in death for his informants. The prostitutes weren't afraid of Crow and had no reason to tell the truth, just as they had no reason to know where Dorothy went. He turned his glare to the brothel and narrowed his eyes. Were they harboring her?

"Coming?" Crow called.

Tin spun to find Crow striding down the street and hurried after him. "You can't believe them without investigating."

"Ah, Tin. Ever the trusting one."

"It's better than trusting everyone."

"Is it?" Crow stared at him with disdain, his brown eyes blazing within his perfectly fitted mask. "Would you like to waste time patting down the nymphs … again, or would you like to find Dorothy before she crosses the border into the South?"

While the East was dangerous, the South was worse, and he had no idea how much of a head start Dorothy had. "You'd better not be wrong about this," Tin growled.

Crow's face grew concerned. "You did warn Dorothy about Langwidere, didn't you?"

"Of course I did," Tin lied, his heart thumping with guilt.

Crossing into southern territory was almost like stepping into another world. A better world, like it used to be the first year after Dorothy returned to Kansas. The yellow brick road wasn't crumbling, and the trees had a bit more life than the ones in the East and West. Even with the violence going on in the South, Glinda had still managed to keep her land from withering as the rest of Oz had. Although it appeared safe, Tin knew Langwidere was still a problem here.

This land harbored the worst kind of danger. The kind that hid and lurked and stalked its prey. Dorothy had no idea of the creatures that prowled here. With her habit of rushing up to any stranger, she was bound to get herself eaten. Or worse. Tin shook the thought from his head.

"If you were Dorothy," Crow began as they passed the pink and gold southern signpost, "where would you go from here?"

"How should I know?"

"You spent the last few days with her, which is more than I have. What's she like?" Crow scratched his head. "Will she wander into the woods or stay to the path?"

Tin dug his knuckles into his eyes and swore under his breath. If Dorothy had veered off the road, there was no telling where she was. She could still be in the East for all they knew. Her sense of direction seemed average for a human, but that wasn't saying much. Tin wanted to tell Crow she would've realized that and stayed on the direct path to the South, but there was every possibility she hadn't. With her being in such a hurry to find Crow, she could've decided to try what she thought was a shortcut, or been led astray by a fae who lied about knowing where Crow was. The sky was the limit with her ignorance. This was partly his fault—he hadn't warned her about Langwidere taking heads in the South.

"I don't know," he finally snapped. His hands fell back to his sides and he huffed, annoyed. "She doesn't seem to have fully grasped how different Oz is now. Being as fearless as she is, she probably walked right up to a goblin to ask for directions."

Crow whipped around to stare at him. "She wouldn't dare approach something so vile. It's suicide."

Tin swung out his arms as if to say: *she would and that's exactly*

86

the problem. "Why don't you shift into your bird form and take a gander from the sky?"

Crow bristled. "Listen, asshole. If I could've had a bird's eye view this whole time, don't you think I would have? Especially if Dorothy's inherited a brain as bad as mine used to be."

"She's a mortal—they're all too dimwitted for their own good," Tin grumbled. They needed to pick up their pace. Scouring the woods in any random direction wasn't going to do them any favors. "Let's just stick to the road for now. Maybe we'll find another town and you can question the locals."

Crow grabbed his elbow and squeezed it. "Dorothy is *not* a mortal."

Tin ripped himself free and laughed. "I see your mind is starting to fade after all. Good on you for keeping some of it this long."

"She's *not* a mortal. And, for the record, my brain is perfectly intact because I took the time to nurture it. You let your heart harden, just as Lion let his courage deprive him of a real connection with anyone."

Crow's words stung. His heart solidified because the world wasn't worth loving, not because he hadn't tended to it. The doors had snapped shut on their own and he hadn't bothered trying to open them again. It hadn't done him any good the first time, and now here the organ was again. Screwing everything up.

But... what if Crow was right? What if the curse returned because he hadn't taken care of his heart? It made sense that it would return now. Someone cared for him for the first time in years. Dorothy thought he was worth something, that he was good and redeemable. She wasn't afraid—she had touched him without hesitation. Ran her fingers gently over his scar.

Tin had heard how love was made of magic—perhaps Dorothy's love broke through the stone walls of his heart. His breath caught. *Love?* What was he thinking? Dorothy didn't *love* him, did she? No. How could she? He wasn't worth something so pure and good. But there were different kinds of love, weren't

87

there? The love of friendship. Which sometimes turned into more over time.

"Fuck my heart. Why the hell is everyone so worried about that?" Tin snarled.

"Perhaps because of all the trouble you went through to *get it?*" Crow waved a dismissive hand through the air. "But you're right. Fuck it. I see the way you're worried about Dorothy, and my daughter deserves better than you."

Tin froze. His daughter? That was impossible. Dorothy grew up in the human world with a human family and an oversized pet rat. Crow wasn't smart enough or strong enough to open a portal and visit Kansas. Maybe his brain was completely gone after all. He didn't remember Crow being delusional before, but then again, Tin hadn't always been a murderer.

"Okay," Tin said slowly. He'd play along until they found Dorothy, then he'd get her as far away from Crow as possible. "Dorothy's half fae… Got it. Can we go now?"

"She's not *half* anything." Crow stormed past Tin.

No, they weren't done yet. Tin followed on his heels. Dorothy looked *nothing* like a fae. Her ears were round, her cheekbones low, though he supposed that could be from her mother's side. But even if it was true—which he doubted—how would Dorothy have made it to Kansas? And why? Crow seemed the type to adore children. He was patient and kind, protective. Fatherly. It didn't make sense for him to give his daughter away, and to mortals no less.

"Who's her mother?" Tin asked slowly, not taking his eyes off Crow.

Crow stumbled again and, instead of answering, pointed ahead. "There's a small settlement over there."

Tin didn't need to hear another word. He broke into a sprint, his heart thundering in his chest. She was there. She had to be. He was too frantic to care that he had feelings for Dorothy— too frantic to know what those feelings were—but he needed to see her. Touch her to confirm she was still all right—safe. It felt like he would combust if he wasted another moment.

A row of pink and purple buildings seemed to scream at him as he stormed into the small town. His limbs shook as he kicked in the door to a bakery. The metallic scent of blood greeted him and he froze. Time seemed to slow as he took in the headless body on the floor.

"No," he whispered to himself.

Not Langwidere. Not here. If Dorothy had come this way, then that meant... Tin's stomach twisted painfully. He bent over, pressing a fist into his abdomen. What was he doing? Bringing Dorothy here? Taking Lion's money for a job like this? He was every bit the monster everyone thought he was. *No. He was worse.*

"The town's been abandoned," Crow said from behind him.

"Not everyone left," he rasped. Even though he'd personally decapitated hundreds of fae, Tin couldn't look at the headless body another second. He knew where Dorothy was. In his gut, *he knew.* "Langwidere was here."

Crow peeked inside the bakery and jerked back. "That's not Langwidere's work."

"Who else do you know that steals heads?" Tin shouted.

Crow's brown eyes met Tin's silver ones with a heavy gaze. They both knew the answer. Langwidere had paraded her prized lover around every chance she got, and Lion seemed to pride himself on helping with Langwidere's unnatural hobby. If anyone knew that, Tin did. He'd sat across the table from Lion and watched the anticipation of getting Dorothy's head spark through his eyes.

"Fuck." Tin's mind swirled with thoughts again. Thoughts he shouldn't have... *Couldn't* have because he didn't care. About anything. Least of all Dorothy. But he realized that was quickly becoming a lie. "*Fuck!*"

"If he harms one hair on my daughter's head, I'll cut his off and shove it down Langwidere's throat," Crow vowed.

The steadiness of his threat made Tin pause. Crow meant that—every word. Whether he was capable of it was another thing, but Tin didn't care. He would cut Lion's head off for Crow if it came down to that. Hell, even if they found Dorothy unscathed, he would swing his axe.

And he wouldn't miss.

CHAPTER TWELVE

DOROTHY

Dorothy couldn't stop thinking about the headless bodies in the shops. The two decaying ones, the skeleton, the dried blood, so much blood. Even the smell lingered in her nostrils, on her clothing. A fae named Langwidere was the cause of this, and she needed to be stopped. Dorothy had a machete, but was that enough? Nothing would compare to the power she'd once possessed when wearing the silver slippers, but those were still gone, lost. Or perhaps ... taken.

A machete could decapitate someone as cleanly as Langwidere's victims, and Dorothy would hack away with it until her dying breath, to save the South.

"Do you know what happened to the silver slippers?" Dorothy turned to Lion, who walked close beside her on the yellow brick road, studying her face as though she might vanish at any moment, or lose her head. She rubbed her neck at the side.

"Slippers?" Lion asked, focusing his attention straight ahead.

"Yes, don't act coy. The slippers that helped me defeat the Wicked Witch, that helped us get our wishes from Oz, the—"

"They no longer exist." He shrugged. "Used up all their power."

Was that even possible? Perhaps it could be since they were only enchanted material. "What about Crow? How's he doing?" He'd been looking for her, and she'd been searching for him. Their paths would hopefully cross soon.

"He's fine. No need to worry." Lion curled a hand around her shoulder, his palm staying there until she pulled out from his grasp.

She hurried in front of him and pressed a hand to his chest, stopping him. "And you? You seem like something's bothering you."

"I'm fine. But of course things are bothering me. You left, remember? The world here has changed … for the worse."

Dorothy frowned. Was everyone mad at her for leaving? She had only been a little girl who'd wanted to go home to her aunt and uncle. Did they not understand that? When the tornado took her, she hadn't gotten to tell Aunt Em or Uncle Henry goodbye. Fear had driven her back home, but that was also the place where she'd felt she needed to be at the time.

"I'm sorry. I always meant to come back, but couldn't find a way. Until now, so I'm here. And I'm here to stay," Dorothy promised. This wasn't the Land of Oz she remembered, but that didn't mean it couldn't be again.

"And stay, you shall." He smiled, but it wasn't a smile she knew from Lion.

Together they continued down the yellow brick road, the sky above them a muted gray, the wind picking up. Ahead sat rows and rows of small pink, green, and blue cottages with thatched roofs. All looked spherical, as though they were bubbles coated in glitter. But there was no sign of anyone outside. A few of the clothing lines were empty—others held garments that appeared to be faded and possibly frayed from weather exposure.

"Where is everyone?" she asked, not taking her eyes from the tiny buildings.

"Most left, some are hiding, others ended up like what you saw at the shops."

Falyn had mentioned that most had fled. Couldn't they have tried fighting back? "But why would Langwidere want to take people's heads. Isn't one good enough?"

Lion chuckled. "She changes them every morning. Sometimes again after dinner, or so they say. When she wears them, she gains the power that those fae once held."

That didn't sound intriguing to Dorothy. It seemed evil, wrong. Aunt Em would have said that the devil himself was upon them, and perhaps she would have been right. As the breeze kicked up even faster, everything else remained quiet. She couldn't hear any sign of life, not even a single bird's chirp or the buzz of insects' wings.

The silence between her and Lion grew more and more uncomfortable. Even with Tin and his broodiness, it had never felt like this. Her shoulders tightened at the strangeness of her surroundings. She found herself missing the Lion from her past. "Why aren't you talking? You always talked. Are you like Tin? Lost a piece of yourself?"

He stopped in his tracks and narrowed his eyes. "Are you implying I'm a coward again?"

"No." She held up her hands. "That's not what I'm saying. I never thought you were a coward to begin with. I mean, you just don't seem yourself." Perhaps she should just stop talking for a while. She was making everything worse.

"You know, I didn't want to have to tell you"—Lion bit his lip and toyed with the end of his tail—"but you shouldn't trust Tin."

Dorothy furrowed her brow—the world seemed to close around her, as if she knew something bad was coming. Like when she'd found out the news about the farm foreclosing. "And why's that? Just because his heart is stone, that doesn't make him malicious—he didn't have a beating one the last time I was here. The Gnome King is to blame for that." He'd kept her safe from the faerie fruit addict on the yellow brick road and the flying fae at night.

"Because he was going to give your head to Langwidere," Lion pursed his lips. He looked as though it haunted him to say the words.

"*What?*" That couldn't be true. There was no way that was possible. "I think you're mistaken, Lion."

"No, Dorothy, I'm not. I can't hide it from you any longer. When I saw him last, he told me his plan and asked me to join in on it. I tried to stop him then, but before my blade could slice his throat, he took off. Even Glinda and Crow want him dead."

"Why would he do that?" Dorothy asked, still in disbelief. But then it truly hit home. Her heart beat rapidly, with the hurt coursing through her veins. "He said you were paying him to bring me to you to help the South."

"Lies. All lies." He waved his hand in the air, a scowl on his face. "You can't trust someone without a beating heart."

She should have known that. Tin had mentioned payment on the journey and how he wouldn't do anything for free. How he'd been paid to kill before. He had been so desperate to bring her to the South. Too desperate. And what was she? Gullible. Naïve. Stupid. It all felt like a kick to the gut. But she wasn't going to let sadness linger—she was growing angrier by the second. If—no, *when*, she ran into Tin again, he would lose something else to go along with his stone heart.

Dorothy peered out toward a small stream trickling in the woods. The exhaustion hit her then. Physically. Emotionally. She'd been up all night traveling, and she needed a break, and something to eat and drink.

"Let's stop here and rest for a bit before we move on," she suggested, heading in the direction of the water.

"No!" Lion shouted from behind her.

She whirled around, scanning the area for any sign of danger. The trees still appeared empty, quiet. "Why not?"

He sauntered up beside her, hand on the blade at his hip.

"Because I need to get you to the palace as soon as possible."

"I need to eat. All I've had were nuts, and I need water. There's a stream right there."

"You'll be fine."

Gripping his arm, she tugged him to the side. "Lion, I need water or I won't be making it to the palace. And even then, I have no power to help the South. The slippers are what helped me before, and now that I don't have them, I'm nothing. Only a woman with a machete, who wouldn't be able to hold her own against a true warrior. So everyone here needs to stop believing that I'm some miracle saint, because I'm not. I'm Dorothy Gale, a farm girl, and that's all I'll ever be. Even then, I may have been stronger as a child when I held hope and believed nothing bad could happen in the world. Your world may have gotten worse, Lion, but so did mine." She tapped a finger fiercely at her chest.

He frowned, but nodded. "I understand."

Tin had been moodier, but he hadn't objected when she'd needed to drink water or relieve herself. Dorothy walked off the yellow brick road and sat at the edge of the narrow stream. She splashed her face with the water and brought handful after handful of cool liquid to her lips.

All along the stream's edge were patches of clovers and tiny colorful orange and yellow flowers. Red and gold fish swam within the stream's depths. Lion pushed his hand in and captured three fish. It took her several tries, but Dorothy grasped a scaly body and tossed it onto the grass. She watched it flip and wiggle before slicing off its head with her machete.

Dorothy and Lion gathered twigs and leaves to build a fire to cook the fish. She ran her hands up and down a stick over the pile. It bit into her flesh as the smoke rose, before the crackling flames took shape. Lion and Dorothy both held their sticks with the fish over the fire, letting it char the meat. Dorothy's came away black, and she blew onto it to cool it down.

"We need to get moving as soon as we finish," Lion said. "I got us these while collecting the sticks. He handed her something yellow and round."

"What is this?" Dorothy asked, inspecting the ridged surface.

"They're a nut that only blooms here in the South. You bite right into it." He rolled the object between his fingertips. "They have a lot of protein, so it will keep your energy up."

"Thanks." Since she'd been here, this was the best meal she'd had. She bit into the fish, and ate all the meat until only bones were left. The bones reminded her of the skeleton inside the shop, and she thrust the remains away from her.

Dorothy remembered when she, Crow, and Tin had stumbled upon Lion for the first time in the woods. Winged beasts had been out, swarming the trees, attacking something with their sharp talons.

Lion had been curled up on his side, filthy, disheveled, not even fighting back. Toto had stood brave and ran toward Lion, barking at everyone, scaring them away. Dorothy had grabbed the male's hand and helped him up, and he'd smiled. For the rest of the journey, Lion held on to Toto and stayed behind Dorothy, as though she was his protector.

"Why haven't you asked about Toto?" Dorothy asked, resting her back against the tree, and bringing the nut in between her lips.

"Who?" He tossed a fishbone to the side. "Oh, the dog. I forgot about him."

Yet Lion still didn't ask about him. Dorothy kept to herself that Toto was dead, because this Lion seemed as if he wouldn't have cared. She took a bite of the nut, but it wasn't hardness she felt. It was soft, juicy. A thin line ran down her chin. Dorothy jerked the nut from her mouth and tossed it to the ground. Her eyes widened and met Lion's golden irises as she spat out the chunk of faerie fruit. "That's not a nut," she breathed. "That's fruit."

Lion rose from the ground, standing above her, his shadow enveloping her. "Oh, my mistake. They may also contain a numbing aid."

Why would you give me a numbing aid? The words came in her head, but her lips wouldn't move for her to speak them aloud. Dorothy's arms grew heavy when she tried to raise them, and her body slumped to the side. Lion scooped her up and held her close. The new smile he'd given her earlier had returned, only this time it became wider, sharper, a smile she didn't know Lion could ever have. As though he were a true lion and she was his prey.

Lion leaned forward, his golden irises flashing. "You once told me fairy tales to build my courage. Remember Snow White? She was never the hero, only a damsel in distress. The witch had truly won, because Snow White did indeed eat the apple. There's no prince here to save you. From your story, I wanted to be more like the Evil Queen, so thank you for that. And thank you for making my job easier after Tin failed. Now, you'll stay silent as I bring you to Langwidere."

Dorothy tried to scream, to reach for her machete, to do *something*, but she couldn't do anything besides watch as Lion started walking her back toward the yellow brick road.

"Close your eyes and rest a bit." He paused then purred, "Oh, you can't close them, can you?" He pressed two fingers to her eyelids and shut them. The only thing left for her to see was darkness.

CHAPTER THIRTEEN

TIN

❦——————❦

Langwidere's residence was a monstrosity. This was where he was supposed to deliver Dorothy to Lion? It kept with the southern architecture but was made entirely of delicately wrought metal. Layers and layers of intricate details formed a globe of tarnished vines with small discolored flowers flowing over the curves. It was every bit as feminine as the rumors of Langwidere herself, and upon closer inspection, nearly as dangerous. Jagged thorns covered the vines and the flower petals were filed to serrated edges.

"Hold on," Crow warned quietly, throwing an arm in front of Tin before he could storm the door. "It's too quiet."

"I think what you mean is *blissfully empty of Dorothy's screams.*" Which meant they needed to hurry, because Tin refused to believe they were too late. Lion only wanted Dorothy for one reason and Tin didn't imagine he would wait long to collect his prize. Crow uttered a soft *shh* and lowered into a crouch just inside the tree line. Tin stared down at him as if seeing him for the first time. "Did ... you just *shush* me?"

"Of course I did." He gripped Tin's wrist and yanked him down beside him. The lawn around Langwidere's palace was cut through with gravel pathways, but was otherwise barren. "It would be more expedient to sneak in unnoticed than to fight whatever Langwidere has guarding this place. She has spies everywhere and probably knows we're coming already."

Tin grunted. He didn't particularly care if he had to slaughter a handful of lesser fae to gain entrance. In fact, he longed for the chance to spill blood, but if the ruckus alerted Langwidere, it could hasten Dorothy's decapitation. Tin grunted again, but this time from the painful coil of dread twisting his stomach.

"Wheelers." Crow bobbed his masked face toward the short stone staircase leading to the front doors. Something glinted beneath the steps.

Tin's hand found his axe. "Screw this."

"Tin, wait!" Crow hissed, but it was too late.

Tin rushed straight for the staircase, ready to swing. The air filled with the high-pitched squeak of rusting wheels. Dozens of Wheelers zoomed toward him, seemingly out of nowhere. The disfigured fae were bent like dogs, their backs arched, a sharp wheel attached to the end of each limb, their mouths stitched shut with bloody white ribbon. Their eyes were bloodshot. Haunted. Crazed. Just as the ones captured and interrogated in the Emerald City were before all hell broke loose.

It wasn't clear who swung first—Tin or one of them—but he was the first to draw blood. A Wheeler's arm came clean off in a spray of ruby blood, and his other wheels wobbled out from under him. Tin was already onto the next before the first hit the ground.

On and on he swung his axe while dodging their blows. One female sped by him and kicked out a razor-sharp wheel as she passed. Tin rolled over the back of another wheeled creature while slicing her leg from knee to ankle. They were no match for him—their strength was in their numbers, but even those were dwindling within the first minute.

99

It wasn't until Tin had dispatched the first round of them, and spun in search of his next target and came up empty, that he realized Crow had helped. How much he had helped was unclear, as he was relatively clean everywhere but his hands. Four silver blades extended from the back of his wrist, previously hidden beneath his bracers, and curved over his hands like talons. When the fuck had he learned how to fight? His best efforts used to be flailing his limbs around.

"I didn't need help." Tin wiped his chin with the back of his hand, smearing the splatter of blood.

Crow stepped over a Wheeler still twitching on the ground. With a heavy sigh, Crow turned around and dealt a final blow through his neck, then headed straight for the front door. "I wasn't helping *you*, you ignoramus."

Shit. Tin took the steps three at a time, his blood-soaked boots slipping slightly against the stone. The door flew open and the stench of decay blasted both Tin and Crow back a step.

"Holy shit," Crow said around a cough.

Tin narrowed his watering eyes and charged inside. "Dorothy! Dorothy, where are you?"

He took in the green and gold interior of the house, putting the layout together, puzzling out where Langwidere might bring someone to kill. Not in her foyer, surely. Carrying her victims upstairs and their bodies back down would be too much work. The heads would be on a higher level—that made the most sense for security. Two massive rooms off the entrance were completely empty of furniture, though one had a large firepit filled with charred crystals. Beyond it, the green floor tiles were broken, as if something had been ripped from the floor. A dark hallway extended further into the dwelling.

"Damn," Crow wheezed through his mask. "It doesn't look like anyone's been here in years."

Tin scowled as the state of the interior sunk in. Cobwebs hung from the ceiling in large sheets. The candles were burnt to nubs, the wax having dripped from the candelabras on the wall to the floor, where a thick layer of dust coated everything.

"I was supposed to bring Dorothy here," Tin said in a rushed breath. There were no footprints on the dusty floor, the cobwebs intact. Something wasn't right. "Langwidere was supposed to be *here*. Lion said... But... I don't understand. They should be here."

The heads. Langwidere wouldn't leave without them. Tin bolted up the staircase and began kicking in ornate doors until he found one filled with glass cases. Empty. Empty. *Empty.* From floor to ceiling, corner to corner, the cases held nothing but dust. His axe fell from his hand with a heavy thump. This couldn't be happening. He gripped the fabric over his beating heart, his iron nails digging into his skin as he fought to breathe.

Dorothy. I'm sorry, Doro—

Crow tackled Tin from behind. They both flew headfirst through a pane of glass. The jagged pieces tore into the scarred side of Tin's face and crunched beneath his boots as he struggled to right himself. Crow's weight held him in place.

"What the hell?" Tin demanded.

One of Crow's hands dug into his hair, grinding Tin's cheek into the rough edge of the broken glass. The iron prevented it from gouging his face in half while the kelpie scales on his clothing stopped the sharp points of Crow's talons from digging into his ribs.

"Give me one reason I shouldn't gut you right here," Crow growled.

Tin gripped the edge of the case and attempted to throw himself backward to gain the upper hand. Crow's talons only shifted higher. "What are you doing?" Tin roared. The movement scratched his bottom lip on a jagged edge. "Let me up, jackass."

Crow's breath was hot on his ear. "Lion hired you to bring my daughter to Langwidere?"

Shit. Tin stilled, letting the pain of his wounds sink in. He deserved this. *More* than this. "If it means anything, I changed my mind the night I overheard you in the brothel."

"You fucked a nymph and decided not to *murder my daughter?* How is that helping your case?"

"I didn't. Fuck the nymph, I mean. I was going to, but then I heard you…" The words tumbled out of Tin before he could stop them. When his mind finally caught up to his mouth, he decided to keep going. If this was it and Crow killed him, at least he would've died with someone knowing the truth. "I didn't want you or anyone else to take her from me. When she woke up, I planned on sending her home. Or letting her stay and protecting her. I don't know, Crow. We didn't get to discuss it because the next morning she was gone. But Langwidere wasn't going to touch her, I swear it."

Tin stopped short of saying he cared for Dorothy. It had to be clear to Crow regardless, and he was still working out exactly what *feelings* meant. He'd never managed to get the hang of them the first time.

"Dorothy's the only one in Oz who would dare to show you compassion after you've killed a friend or relative of damn near everyone here," Crow said in a low, guttural voice. He dragged his talons to Tin's chest and pressed them where Tin's heart was beating. "I see your heart has returned. But it doesn't matter, Tin, because you've broken hers as much as you've broken my trust."

"Dorothy's kindness broke my curse." Tin sighed miserably. "She doesn't know what Lion hired me for."

Crow shoved Tin deeper onto the broken glass as he released him. Tin sagged to the floor, defeated, and Crow kicked his axe toward him. "She *will* know."

"You're not going to kill me?" Tin wiped the blood trickling from his cut lip. "I deserve it."

"Oh, you will die," Crow promised. "But first you're going to fix this. You're going to use that cruelty of yours and thirst for blood to save my daughter, then you're going to tell her the truth. After, Dorothy will decide your fate."

With that, Crow spun on his heel and stormed from the

abandoned building. Tin climbed slowly to his feet, dragging his axe up behind him.

Ah, he thought. *There's an emotion I remember.*

The shattering pain in his chest could be nothing other than heartbreak.

When they found Dorothy, when Lion and Langwidere were dead and Dorothy heard of his betrayal, he hoped she would be the one to end his suffering. Though perhaps letting him live would be the harsher punishment.

Chapter Fourteen

Dorothy

———◆———

Dorothy stood in the center of a silver garden. A rocky circular path enveloped her, blooming tall with flowers of the same sparkling sheen. This world was completely gray. From behind a looming tree of iron came a shadow, a cloaked figure. He removed his dark hood from his head, his silver hair flapping in the wind. The purest eyes of silver she'd ever seen connected with hers. Tin.

He sauntered toward her, smiling that smile he'd worn before she'd returned to Kansas. The branch-like scars running down his cheek glistened beneath the sun and her heart sped up. He was the most beautiful thing she'd ever seen.

Dorothy inched closer, closer, until his hand came to her lower lip in a soft brush.

Tin's head leaned down to kiss her but before his mouth touched hers, his lips moved close to her ear, to where she'd felt his warm breath. "Sorry, Dorothy."

There wasn't enough time for her to think as he stepped back. Lion shifted out from behind a tree, nodding at Tin. Her eyes widened as Tin's hands arched up, swinging his axe. Her feet stayed planted in the dirt of the garden, unable to move as the blade bit into her neck and sailed through, spraying the silver garden in a sea of scarlet.

Dorothy woke up screaming—screaming so terribly loud. But only in her head. Even inside there, it splintered her eardrums. She couldn't bring her lips to part. She couldn't move anything.

Two fingers drew her eyelids open. Her pupils took a moment to adjust to the new lighting. All Dorothy could do was watch the parts of the world above her move—the blue sky, the fluffy clouds, tops of colorful trees, and part of a fur cloak. *Lion.* The bastard.

How could he do this? *Why* would he do this? She shouldn't have been this stupid. It was because she'd known him before, had trusted him.

"I can tell you're awake now." Lion's voice boomed from above her, but she couldn't see his face. "I can see your eyes twitching." He adjusted her body so that his golden irises appeared in front of her. "I'm not doing this because I don't like you, Dorothy. Although, I don't care for you anymore, not since you left. I'm doing this for Langwidere. Your head will look much better on her body, anyway. Until we get there, I'll tell you stories, like you used to tell me to keep me calm."

Dorothy tried to scream again, but nothing came out.

The stories Lion started to tell her weren't ones as she'd told him from *Grimms' Fairy Tales*. These were stories that truly sickened her, because they were real.

"I began collecting heads for Langwidere years ago. She tested me the first time in her old home, where I was given the opportunity to decapitate a female she had tied up in another room. I completed the task, and you know what? It felt good—more than good—especially when she fucked me for the first time right afterward. It became a ritual for us. I'd kill a female, then she'd reward me with a fuck."

Lion didn't stop there. He continued on and on, about each of his kills, about the different heads Langwidere wore while he bedded her, and how sometimes there was blood in between their naked bodies while he slid inside her. Dorothy had never wanted to have her ears cut off, or her eardrums removed, more in her life than in that moment. She didn't want to hear about how Lion pleased Langwidere sexually or how he relished hearing the victims beg and plead before slicing off their heads. Some of the females they left tied up for days, others weeks, and some they let run so he could play a game of cat and mouse.

As Lion continued, Dorothy didn't understand why the faerie fruit wasn't affecting her the way it should have been. There should have been hallucinations, which would have been better than listening to Lion. But she wasn't feeling a high and she wasn't going crazy. There was only the numbing sensation, holding her body still.

Something thrummed in Dorothy's veins then. It was familiar, achingly familiar, but it couldn't be. It was the same inner strength she'd dredged up when she'd worn the silver slippers and used their power, except she wasn't wearing the shoes now. Dorothy's veins pulsed harder, almost like they were stirring up a tinge of magic. And now the hallucinations were starting—of that she was certain.

The rapture was coming, and she feared there would be no turning back. She was going to become a faerie fruit addict— deranged like the man who'd attacked her on the yellow brick road, or insane like Oz. Yearning and yearning for each precious bite of fruit while it blackened her teeth and tickled her insides. She would never be able to think clearly again—she'd be positively mad like the Mad Hatter from her favorite childhood story.

For a moment, Dorothy gave in to the hallucination, tried reaching into herself with invisible hands, pretended as though she was wearing the silver slippers. Her invisible fingers brushed against something not quite tangible. Clearer and clearer it became. Inside her shell of a body, she tightened her grip on a flexible surface, and before her, the bright glow of silver flared to life, like that of the slippers.

Dorothy's body stopped moving. Lion had halted, staring down at her, his voice appearing far away as he shouted, "What the fuck?"

Deeper and deeper she tapped into the silver, as deep as she could go. Like a shooting star, something within her—perhaps magic—exploded outward. Lion was shot backward and Dorothy fell on her back against the hard ground. Pain radiated up her spine.

A roar slipped out from her throat, echoing throughout the forest beside the yellow brick road.

Lion came to a crouch and slowly stood, staring at her in horror. A silvery glow expanded around her.

"Locasta wasn't lying. She spoke the truth about you," And instead of coming after her with his sword, the coward took off running in the opposite direction.

Dorothy's eyes fluttered as she reached for her machete, her body tingling with needle-like pricks. A sharp pain tore at the tips of her ears—she touched them and gasped. They weren't rounded any longer, but sharpened points, like those of elves. Her trembling hands automatically crawled to her face, skimming her cheekbones. They'd shifted higher.

What is happening?

With wide eyes, Dorothy peered around, needing to flee. She didn't know where in the South she was exactly. But she did know Lion wasn't with Glinda or Crow now. He was with Langwidere. She couldn't go back to Tin because he was trying to bring her to this bitch who took heads for her own sick pleasure. And she didn't know which path to follow on the yellow brick road to get to Glinda.

Farther back stood a cluster of tiny yellow and orange homes, resembling lemons and oranges with stacks of large brown leaves forming the roofs. She hurried in that direction, toward a short green fence enclosing all the houses.

When she entered the gate, multiple mounds in the earth

caught her attention. Dorothy slowed her pace. In a grassy area filled with clovers, and tiny white flowers, rested cemetery markers. Written across each one was a female's name—there wasn't a single male's name. A sinking feeling washed over Dorothy. A few of the graves appeared fresh with exposed dirt but others were already grown over with grass. Whirling around, she took off toward the first house and banged on the door.

"You shouldn't be out here like this," a male voice called from a few cottages down. She turned in that direction and moved toward the satyr, until she came face to face with him. The top of his head came to her chest, and he appeared mostly goat-like, with horns, a tail, and hooves. Bright violet irises shone beneath the sun.

"I need your help," Dorothy said, trying not to sound desperate or look crazed as she gripped her machete.

The satyr waved her hurriedly inside his home. She didn't move toward it.

"I'm not going to hurt you." He sighed. "You shouldn't be out here like this. It's safe for us males but not the females, especially ones who look like you."

"What's wrong with me?" she asked, deciding it was better to go inside in case Lion did choose to return and search for her.

"There's nothing wrong with you. Langwidere simply favors elves with pretty faces. I'm sure you've already passed the grave markers. They all lost their heads because of her."

This Langwidere was starting to sound like the Headless Horseman from the Sleepy Hollow story, except she actually wore the heads. Dorothy shuddered at the thought.

As she stepped inside the satyr's home, she entered a small dining room area with a wooden kitchen table and two chairs. Two empty vases sat on the counter in the corner as if they'd once contained flowers. She took a seat in a chair and he sank down in the other.

Dorothy's eyes met the satyr's bright violet ones. She thought about his previous words and they struck her right then.

"You mentioned Langwidere favors pretty elves, but I'm human."

His brow furrowed and his nose wrinkled. "You're not human. You're fae."

Dorothy froze, a cold feeling washing over her, spreading through her entire body. "Listen, I'm Dorothy Gale. I came here once before, and I'm human. Lion did something to me." Her chest heaved up and down as her heart raced. "What did that fruit do to me?"

"Um, let me get you some tea." He stood from the table, picked up a tea kettle off the stove, and poured them both a cup. "I know who you are, but I don't have the answers you're searching for."

As he handed her the cup of steaming tea, she tipped it back and took a sip, wishing she had something stronger. The liquid burned her throat as it slid down, but the burn felt good, nonetheless. "Do you have a mirror?"

"Yes, let me see what I can do." The satyr left her sitting there, nervously tapping her fingers on the table. Right as she was about to go searching for a mirror herself, he slipped back into the kitchen area holding a small oval one with intricate vine engravings around the glass.

Despite wanting to rip the mirror from his grasp, she gently took it from the satyr's fingers and held it up to her face. As she observed herself, her hands shook more. The tips of her ears were indeed pointed, eyes larger, cheekbones higher. She calmly set the mirror face down, as if nothing about her had changed. She didn't want to look at herself anymore.

"Can you please tell me how to get to Glinda's from here?" she asked, taking another sip of the herbal tea, the drink sloshing in the cup as her hands vibrated.

"By foot, it's a few days' journey from here—at the very bottom of the South in front of the mountains." He paused, his expression grim. "However, I suggest going to one of the other territories instead. Glinda is a great leader and has been doing all

109

she can to save the South, but Langwidere is growing stronger, more powerful."

"I still have to go. Glinda is a friend." Dorothy needed to warn her about Lion and Tin, that they were traitors.

"Let me at least feed you first." Before she could reply, the satyr plopped down a plate in front of her with a meat pie on top. Her stomach rumbled as she peered down at the golden layers of the delicacy. Whatever she'd done to Lion had taken a lot of her energy. She dug in like a ravenous beast.

"Thank you... I'm sorry, I didn't ask your name," she said.

"Tigue." He smiled. "I've believed this entire time that Glinda would defeat Langwidere, but maybe she just needs your help. You are Dorothy Gale, after all, the one who took down the wickedest of them all."

Dorothy's chest sank, but she smiled in return. She thought about the fae and how, if someone spoke their full name, they could be controlled. When he'd just said her full name, she didn't feel a tug or buzz of anything. She couldn't be fae. There was no way possible. So, whatever was going on with her had to be temporary—it *had* to be.

After she finished eating, Tigue walked Dorothy outside and pointed her in the direction of a cluster of tall mountains far in the distance. "Be safe, Dorothy Gale."

To be extra careful, she stayed off the yellow brick road, near the outskirts of the forest. If she lingered on the road, she would have stood out like a beacon. She didn't know if Lion would be prowling about or if he'd continue to be a coward and run back to Langwidere.

Rows and rows of bright red apples hung from the leafy tree limbs. Even though she'd just eaten, they looked delicious. However, as she trekked down the bumpy path, she left them alone, in case none of this was truly real.

Near a fork in the road, voices came spiraling from her left. She scrambled and ducked behind a wide trunk covered in thick moss. As she peeked her head slowly around the side, the voices

110

drew closer—male. Two of them. What if Lion had come back with a friend to help him collect her? Craning her neck, she listened closely. The travelers seemed to be arguing, and neither one had the soft voice of Lion.

As two cloaked figures came around a curve, Dorothy identified one immediately. She knew his broad shoulders, his steady gait, and the silver shining out from his hood. *Tin.* Her traitorous heart sped up at the sight of him until she remembered that he was a betraying bastard. But her lips parted when her gaze focused on his companion. She recognized the beaked mask, the sway of his cloak, the thin ropes draped across his bare chest, and his long dark hair braided with feathers. Crow. Tin was with *Crow.*

Did this mean that Tin was tricking Crow, or that Crow was helping Tin and Lion?

The pads of Dorothy's fingers rapidly beat against the moss. She didn't know what to do. Should she make herself known, or just let them pass and hurry to find Glinda?

"You'll be dead after we find Dorothy," Crow seethed. "I can't believe you would try to do something so foul to her."

At Crow's words, Dorothy sighed in relief because, for once, someone was on her side. Her attention went back to Tin, and her blood started to boil, because she'd liked him, really liked him. Had even felt something for him, despite him having a stone heart. *Well, not anymore.*

Ripping her machete free at her back, Dorothy jumped out from behind the tree and barreled for Tin. Before he could whirl around, she leapt onto his back and pushed him roughly to the bricked road. He quickly rolled over beneath her, but she shoved him down, his face full of surprise. Dorothy got in position, straddling his hips, her blade to his throat. "It looks as though you'll be the one losing your head," she spat. "Not me."

CHAPTER FIFTEEN

TIN

Tin's breath caught in his throat. *Dorothy?* It couldn't be. She looked so different ... so *fae*. If she was beautiful before, she was strikingly gorgeous now. Her new fae features practically glowed with radiance. Even her body felt different as she straddled him—more lithe. But how? What caused these changes?

The prick of her machete against his neck sent Tin careening back to reality, and he met her haughty gaze. Hatred swirled in her eyes, the sentiment echoing on her snarling lips, and he fell utterly limp beneath her. Lion must've told her the truth. There was no doubt she'd met with him—Lion's earthy scent still lingered on her. But where was he now? The machete bit harder into his skin, painfully refocusing his attention on the deadly situation.

"If it's my head you want," he rasped, "it's yours. I won't fight you."

Confusion flickered through Dorothy's expression. "What?"

"It's no less than I deserve." Tin lifted his chin to give her better access. When she didn't move to strike, he closed a hand around hers, on the handle of the machete, pressing the blade deeper into his skin. A trickle of warm blood leaked down his throat. "Go on."

Dorothy launched herself off him with heavy breaths. "What is *wrong with you?*"

Tin sat up slowly, every muscle aching, and exhaled. *Fuck.* The infamous Tin Man was *not* going to be taken out by Crow. One way or another, Dorothy had to do it.

Dorothy paced away from him, then back, three times before turning her gaze to Crow. "He was going to kill me," she told him as if to justify her actions. "Lion paid him to bring me to Langwidere so she could wear my head."

Crow nodded. "I recently became aware."

Tin shifted onto his knees. "I can explain."

"*Explain?*" she shouted. "What is there to explain? You were going to let them cut off my head! My *head*, Tin!" She tapped at her skull several times as though to prove it was still there. "You're as stone-hearted as you told me you were."

Tin wanted to tell her that he wasn't—not anymore. That he could feel his heart beating in his chest again, and all the emotions that went along with it, but it didn't matter. He'd messed up. "I wasn't going to let Lion take you, not anymore," he said quietly. "Please believe me."

"Believe you?" Dorothy laughed bitterly. "I was the only one who *trusted* you, but I see now it was foolish of me to do so."

Tin climbed to his feet and moved toward her, but Crow stepped between them. "I told you that she would decide who ended your life. If she won't do it—" Crow flicked his wrist and his talons shot out over his hand, the metal glistening under the sun.

Dorothy's eyes widened. "This isn't your battle, Crow. Have you lost your mind?" Her hands flew to her mouth. "Oh no. You have, haven't you?"

Crow removed the mask from his face. "I haven't lost my brain. In fact, I've expanded it with years of study. Something

I've come to learn is that a little violence to save lives is better than pacifism that leads to hundreds of deaths."

"He's not going to kill hundreds of people," Dorothy grumbled, seemingly against her will. "Just me, apparently, and whoever got in the way of his payday."

Tin swallowed hard at her defense. He didn't deserve it, even if she was wrong about him killing her. That was never the plan—Lion asked for her to be brought alive. He or Langwidere were going to do the killing, but he would've facilitated it, which was almost the same thing.

"He's already killed hundreds," Crow said. "If not more."

It was definitely more, but he didn't dare say as much. Each death weighed on him now. It was a crushing force, one that almost made him wish for the oblivion Crow wanted to give him. Almost. But, while he deserved it, while he knew it was the fastest way to stop feeling this pain, he also knew there was no going back from death. Tin wasn't sure he could change. Bloodlust was ingrained in him now, but he could continue fighting it. And if Dorothy could find it in herself to forgive him, maybe he wasn't a lost cause.

Or maybe he had been right all along: his heart was never a gift from the Wizard. It was a curse.

"I don't care, Crow," Dorothy said. "We aren't killing him, because that would make us as bad as him."

"We aren't being conniving about it," Crow reasoned. "It would be a practical kill."

Conniving was a strong word. Appropriate this once, but Tin didn't feel it accurately described him in general. There wasn't much scheming that went into assassinations. The customer paid, his axe swung. The targets always knew what was about to happen if they saw him.

"No," Dorothy insisted.

Crow pressed his lips into a tight line and retracted his talons. "As you wish."

Her shoulders slumped with exhaustion, the immediate

danger gone. A smile broke across her face and she lunged at Crow. She wrapped her arms around his neck in the biggest hug. "It's so good to see you."

"And you." Crow returned the hug without hesitation. "I missed you."

Tin rolled his eyes as Crow spun her around, her feet lifting off the ground. "As touching as this reunion is, there seems to be a rather glaring issue to discuss."

The smile slipped from Dorothy's lips in an instant and she stepped away from the embrace. "You mean my face?"

Crow studied her, taking in each feature as if he'd never see them again. A peaceful expression fell over his features each time his eyes returned to Dorothy's new, high cheekbones. "Your glamour's gone. You look like—" He quickly cleared his throat. "What happened?"

"I don't know... I had a glamour?" Her fingers skimmed the lines of her new face, then the tips of her pointed ears. "Lion found me. He said you were with Glinda, and Tin had told me we were going to Lion's to help him, so I followed him. He tricked me into eating faerie fruit with numbing properties. When I regained use of my body, it had changed. Is ... this an effect of the fruit?"

"No, sweetheart." Crow paused and fidgeted with the ropes hanging down his chest. "You're fae. A changeling who was glamoured to live among humans."

Tin exhaled impatiently. "If we're having this conversation here, let's cut straight to the point so we can get somewhere safe. Crow's your father." Both Crow and Dorothy's eyes widened in shock. Tin ignored the jolt of guilt their expressions sparked. "Now that we've got it out in the open, we need to get the hell out of the South."

"You're my *father*?" Dorothy asked in a hoarse whisper.

Crow nodded, his throat bobbing. Had the bastard been planning on keeping it a secret? Too bad. "You were taken from your mother and I. Once the Wizard corrected my brain and I remembered, it felt wrong to keep you here. You were safer there with the family you'd been given to."

Tin shuffled down the yellow brick road, hoping they would take the hint and talk as they walked. Neither moved. *Fine.* They could stand there and let Lion track them down, but Dorothy had better not ask Tin to let him live.

"Taken? Who is my mother?" Dorothy whispered. "I was always told my parents were dead. Is she… Is she dead? She must not be if you're here."

Crow swallowed hard. "Forgive me, but I'm not ready to tell you yet."

Tin rapped his fingers on the head of his axe, the iron tips clicking loudly, but no one seemed to notice. "We're running out of daylight," he called, agitated. Dorothy would *unquestionably* ask him not to kill Lion, and he wasn't ready to let her down again so soon.

"Let's find somewhere to camp then. You look exhausted." Crow spoke to Dorothy but shot Tin a scathing look. "After you rest, I'll be happy to answer all your questions."

Dorothy nodded, appearing in shock, then jumped away from Crow. "We can't go back to the East. We need to help Glinda. What if Lion tries to do something to her after tricking her?"

"Glinda has been holding her own," Crow soothed.

"And she has guards. Lion won't stand a chance on his own," Tin agreed. "Our priority is keeping you safe."

Dorothy adjusted the machete on her back. She hadn't once looked at Tin—it was as though he wasn't even there. "If that's true—"

The way she spoke was an accusation of a lie, and Tin dropped his gaze.

"—then you'll follow me to Glinda's, because I'm going."

Tin's head fell back with a groan. *Not this again.* She couldn't be this eager to die. Not after how angry she'd gotten at him for working with Lion. Why wouldn't she just *listen?* He ran his hands through his hair, the bone rings on one side catching on his iron-tipped gloves. How had his life become … this?

"Coming?" she called, heading farther south on the brick road.

Suddenly feeling as tired as Dorothy looked, Tin pulled his hood high over his head, hiding his shame. He would make this up to Dorothy. First by killing Lion and Langwidere; then, he suspected, by exiting her life forever.

They had only walked twenty minutes before stumbling upon an abandoned house. Pastel green paint peeled away and what was once a barn off to one side had collapsed, but the house offered shelter. Shelter that they might not find again if they continued traveling, so after some careful urging on Crow's part, they barricaded themselves inside with old furniture. Tables and chairs went against the door while large pieces such as the hutch cupboard covered the windows.

Tin sat quietly at the edge of the former sitting room, cleaning dried blood from his axe, while Crow continued answering Dorothy's questions on what it meant to be fae. She was now able to hear and see better. Move faster. Her body was more in tune with the world around them—something that Crow claimed might be overwhelming until she got used to it. She would age differently now. Immortality and all benefits. Maybe she inherited Crow's gift of shifting, but it was too soon to try.

Tin wasn't sure how many times Dorothy needed to hear the same thing in different words for them to sink in, but they had more pressing things to discuss. But, by some miracle, he held his tongue.

Eventually they moved away from the changes to Dorothy's body to the current state of Oz and what they'd both been doing for the last decade. Dorothy lost her mortal family, her dog, her farm, while gaining a reputation for being insane. Crow had studied every book at the library and looked for fae he'd forgotten about while cursed, though most had completely disappeared. It seemed to Tin that they were equally lost and lonely.

Maybe all of them were, Lion included. Was that what led to their individual demises? The *need* for a sense of belonging like the four of them had while traveling together? None of them appeared to have found it again until, perhaps, now.

Tin waited and waited for them to run out of things to talk about. Or, even better, for them to circle back around to their biggest threat. It wasn't until Dorothy began talking about flying monkeys that he lost any semblance of patience.

"They aren't flying monkeys! The night beasts are cursed pixies." Tin slammed his axe down. "Are we going to talk about Langwidere?"

"Tin," Crow warned, extending his talons. Tin didn't give two shits about those blades. He'd chop them off with his axe if Crow tried anything.

Dorothy placed a hand on Crow's arm. "No. He's right. It's not enough to warn Glinda about the threat. We have to do more and help her fight."

"She's going to have more Wheelers." Crow leaned toward Dorothy. "Wheelers are fae that Langwidere rescued from the Deadly Desert in exchange for their servitude. She replaced their hands and feet with wheels and sewed their mouths shut. We had to dispatch some while searching Langwidere's for you."

Dorothy paled. "Was Langwidere home?"

"No one's been there in years, judging by the state of it," Crow said.

"If Langwidere isn't living there, where *is* she living?" Dorothy looked over her shoulder toward the table they'd placed in front of the door.

"Good question," Tin said. If they made it to Glinda's palace in one piece, maybe they would find out. Glinda was a simpleton, but the fae around her weren't. Someone had to know where Langwidere was, especially if she was still actively collecting heads.

When Dorothy yawned, Crow stood and offered her his hand. "None of us will be any good if we don't sleep."

Dorothy let him help her to her feet and guide her to one of the bedrooms. He opened the door for her and entered first, doing yet another sweep for danger. He'd never seen Crow act like this. Kind, always, pompous, yes, but this mother hen act was new. Was this what happened when one became a parent? Thank goodness he'd never procreated. Crow shook the massive wardrobe in front of the window, testing its strength, and Tin's upper lip lifted. What is she? An infant? Crow didn't need to check for monsters under the bed—they'd already made sure the house was clear. Let the girl sleep. No, not a girl, a *female*. A fae.

When Crow was finally satisfied, he ushered Dorothy farther into the room. "Do you need anything? I can go out to scavenge for some food and fill our canteens. Oh! There's bound to be extra blankets somewhere."

"Stars above, Crow. Leave her alone!" Tin put the axe back on his hip and paced the room.

"Goodnight," Dorothy said gently to Crow, then shot Tin a stern look.

"Sleep well," Crow replied. "Don't worry about Lion or Tin. I'll make sure you're safe."

Tin looked away to keep from snarling in Crow's direction. He wouldn't hurt Dorothy, but if he was planning to escape with her, there wasn't much Crow could do to stop him. With his weapon clean, Tin settled down on the floor to one side of Dorothy's door for the night and stared up at the ceiling.

"You can take one of the other bedrooms," Crow grumbled.

Tin closed his eyes and tucked his hands beneath his head as a pillow. "It's all yours."

Dorothy sighed heavily and slammed the door, shutting them both out. Crow stepped over Tin, kicking him in the process, and sprawled out on the moth-eaten couch. It didn't take long for his breath to even out.

Some guard you are.

From the other side of the door, Dorothy sniffled. Tin leaned up on his elbows and listened harder. Was she … crying? *Shit.* He'd had his heart back for all of one day. The instinct to cheer her up warred with his usual response to emotions: ignoring them. Easing to his feet, eyes glued on Crow, he cursed himself. It seemed he couldn't help trying, but he braced himself for her instant rejection.

And then there was the fight he would have with Crow when her screams woke him.

With a sigh, he slipped quietly into the room. "Dorothy?"

"What do *you* want?" The soft light of dusk filtered through the windows of the small room, a glow sneaking around their barricades.

Tin eased down on the foot of the bed while she sat at the other end with her knees pressed against her chest. "Are you okay?"

"What do you think?" she snapped.

"I think, with your glamour gone, you can do anything you want—*be* anyone you want." She could make an entirely new life for herself if she chose.

"I could be Langwidere," she hissed. "Or I suppose she could be *me.*"

Tin winced at the anger in her words. "I wasn't going to give you to Lion."

"*Liar.*"

He *was* a liar. When he'd opened that portal and dragged Dorothy back to Oz, he'd had every intention of delivering her for a huge sum. "I *was* but I changed my mind once I spent time with you."

Dorothy grunted. "I don't trust you."

"I know," he said softly. When Dorothy sniffled again, burying her face in her knees, Tin laid down on the bed. He

120

stretched out with false confidence. His shoulder brushed her hip and he soaked in that small touch. "This is more comfortable than the floor."

"There's a perfectly good couch," she deadpanned.

"Ah, yes. But your father happens to be out cold on it."

Dorothy shifted to glare at him. "There's another bedroom."

"It's too cold," he lied. He hadn't even looked inside while Crow secured it.

Dorothy pushed his chest with her foot. "You can't stay in here."

"Why not?" He caught her ankle gently. "We've slept next to each other every night since you came back."

"Because you *were going to have me decapitated, you bastard!*" She was angry, but she didn't reach for her weapon, didn't try to shove him again.

Tin tugged her down beside him, suppressing the fear that she would scream for Crow, and wrapped an arm around her waist. When she did nothing but tense against him, he shivered. He wanted to pull her closer but knew not to push his luck. "I'm sorry, Dorothy. But I'm different now."

Dorothy laughed bitterly. "You're so full of shit."

Tin took her hand and pressed it over his heart. Then he waited. Waited for her to *feel* it, to understand what it meant.

"Your heart," she whispered, her eyes full of wonder. "It's beating. How?"

He exhaled a laugh. "It seems you've broken my curse."

"What?" she asked, almost as if she hadn't heard.

"You still believed in me when no one else in this wretched land would. Because you cared about me, because you didn't give up despite everything, your compassion helped to break my heart from its stone prison."

Dorothy's eyes glistened. "I—"

"It's yours," he vowed. "You resurrected my heart when I thought it was gone forever, so its fate is yours. Rip it out and burn it to ash if that makes you happy. But know this: no matter how long you allow me to keep it, I will cherish this gift and use it to protect you."

"Wow." Dorothy scrunched her nose. "So dramatic, Tin. Who knew hearts came with a heaping side of valor?"

Tin gave her a small grin. "Enough of that, then. No more tears and no more talking. We both need to sleep."

Instead of pushing him away as he expected, Dorothy set her head on his chest and snuggled against his side with a contented sigh. She tucked a hand beneath her chin, right over the powerful *thump, thump, thump* of his heart. "Don't think this means I forgive you."

Tin's eyes drifted shut as he inhaled the light feminine scent wafting up from her. It was one of the things about her that had stayed the same. With her hand over his chest, a thirst began to spread through him, igniting everywhere. "I wouldn't dare think that."

But he knew she hadn't heard him. Her head had already gone heavy against his chest as she gave in to her exhaustion. Tin smiled against her hair and held her even closer as he followed suit.

CHAPTER SIXTEEN

DOROTHY

Squeak. Squeak. Squeal. Dorothy's eyes flew open when she heard another loud squeak, her heart thumping in her chest too fast for its own good. In her arms, she gripped something hard, firm—Tin. He was holding on to her just as tight. Before she could say anything, his hand came up and wrapped around her mouth. And at that moment, she knew she shouldn't have trusted him. Once a liar always a liar—heart or not.

He inched his mouth right beside her ear and whispered, "Shh, they'll hear."

She shouldn't have jumped to conclusions, but how could she not have after everything? Dorothy slowly nodded, and Tin released his calloused palm from her lips. In a quiet, yet deadly way, he stood from the bed and grabbed his axe, carefully creeping to the window. He held out a palm for her to remain there. She wasn't going to listen to him.

Silently rising from the bed, she pressed her bare feet to the cool floor and picked up her machete.

When he heard her steps, he shot her a hard glare, but didn't say anything as she sidled up beside him. Peering around his wide form, and between the slit of the barricade they'd put up, she caught glimpses of shadowy figures passing quickly by their shelter. Clusters and clusters of them as though they'd never end. All she could make out clearly under the moon's yellow light were silvery wheels. *Wheelers.*

Dorothy had never encountered one before. In the dark, she was unable to see the ribbons that sewed their mouths shut. What kind of person sewed mouths shut and took heads? Langwidere and Lion might not be difficult to kill since there were only two of them, but an entire clan of Wheelers was a different story.

"What are they doing?" Dorothy asked softly, shifting back so she was pressed against the wall.

"Your guess is as good as mine, but I assume searching for more heads."

"Or searching for *my* head." Her grip tightened against the handle of the machete. "There are too many for us to fight if they come in here." Tin might be good with an axe, but how long would he last? And Crow's finger blades could take down a few, but not all. Then there was Dorothy's experience, taking down … *corn…*

"They don't know we're here." Tin stepped away from the wall and tugged Dorothy back by her sleeve.

Instead of laying back down in bed, Dorothy headed into the sitting room to check on Crow. On the couch, he rested curled up on his side, arm hanging over the edge, and still passed out like a baby. *Her father.* He was her father…

She was still confused, with too many questions and not enough answers. But even when he hadn't remembered her, when she'd just met him, there had been something between them. He'd held her hand when she'd missed her family. She'd felt closer to him than anyone. And now she understood why.

Someone had taken her from her parents, and she hadn't pushed him about it, but she would have to soon.

Dorothy shrugged off whatever she was feeling, set down her machete, and slid back into bed, unable to return to sleep. Tin climbed in beside her, and neither of them spoke. After everything, she was still angry, and he wasn't forgiven. But, perhaps he eventually could be. Dorothy was good with forgiveness—Aunt Em had taught her that. Aunt Em... Uncle Henry... Neither one was real family, but they still felt like it, would always be. And she'd forgiven them, after they'd hurt her, too. Instead of believing her, they'd had her poked and prodded. Too many memories of needles and experiments. Perhaps there was a reason why she wasn't permanently damaged by it all, because she was fae. Not human.

Crow said he hadn't come back for her once he remembered because he thought she was better off. But had she been? She had no doubt that Aunt Em and Uncle Henry had both loved her, but they should have tried to believe her.

"You look like you're thinking too hard," Tin said, interrupting Dorothy's thoughts.

"Because I am." Her frown deepened as she thought about something else. She remembered the short chat she'd had with the satyr. "I don't even think Dorothy Gale is my true name."

"You would feel it if it was. Fae know."

Her head turned in his direction, but she couldn't make out his expression in the dark. "What is it?"

"I wouldn't know. Crow or your mother will know your first name. Your true full name is something you're born with and have to tap into."

Closing her eyes, Dorothy tried to tap into that bit of silver she'd been able to get to with Lion when she'd broken out from her glamour. Digging and digging, she couldn't feel it, couldn't see it. "I can't."

"Don't worry about it." Tin shifted closer, his arm almost brushing hers. "If you don't know your true name, then no one else can know it either. You wouldn't want to be controlled by another."

Something struck her then, and her heart dropped into her stomach. "Have you been controlled before?"

He shook his head. "No one knows my true name except for me, but I've seen it happen to others."

Relaxing her shoulders, she leaned back into her pillow. "It's a good secret to keep."

Tin blew out a huff of air and groaned, as if he was struggling with himself whether to speak or not. "When you went back to Kansas, I truly smiled for the first time. Not because I was given my heart, but because I knew you would go on to do great things. Your heart was always good, selfless and kind. It still is. And now that you're back, you're someone new, different. It's like we're meeting for the first time, you know?"

"I guess?" Dorothy did know, because she was seeing him through a woman's eyes now, not a girl's. Even though she wasn't technically a 'woman' anymore, she still felt like one.

"I know I'm getting too fucking deep here," he said. "But if I tell you my name, would you forgive me?"

The edges of Dorothy's lips tilted up. "Are you trying to barter with me?"

"No. It's just, if you can control me, then you can order me not to harm you. You'll never have to worry about—"

Dorothy's eyes widened and she flung her body forward, pressing her hand to his lips and straddling his hips. "I trust you." She threw the words out and smiled. "I forgive you. But if you betray my trust again, my machete will be put to use, just as your axe has been."

As she removed her palm from his mouth, her cheeks reddened because she was still cradling his hips ... again. Why did she keep finding herself in this predicament with him? Before she could remove herself from him, Tin wrapped his strong arms around her and leaned forward. The words came out in a rush as he whispered them at her ear, his breath tickling her flesh. "Tarragontin Aodh Greenbriar."

Realizing what he'd just done, Dorothy inhaled sharply and

lifted her hands to shove him for being so stupid. But he was fast, and he gripped her wrists, smiling. *Smiling*. And even in the dark, she could see that frustrating smile, the same one he'd given her before she'd left the Land of Oz.

He'd believed in her then, and he believed in her now.

Her shoulders relaxed and she leaned forward. Tin released her wrists, allowing her to wrap her arms around him. At his ear, she murmured, "I promise I won't ever tell anyone or use it against you."

He embraced her back, and mumbled beautiful words at the crook of her neck, "You may use me however you wish."

The sentence sank in, leaving Dorothy to focus on just how close their bodies were. Her chest heaved up and down, up and down. His breaths sounded hard, ragged. Reclining backward, she should have removed her legs from his hips—she didn't. Instead, she let her forehead kiss his in a warming touch. Lips. His lips were so close, his breath now mingling with hers, kissing there too. Everything was kissing except for their lips, and she wanted them to kiss, needed them to. As if under a spell, she angled her head to the side, and her lips finally pressed against his soft mouth.

Dorothy brought her hand to his iron scar, her fingers lightly touching the raised ridges. The warmth tingled her skin, and she wondered how often he felt pain from the scar, but she didn't ask and she didn't pull away from him. He inhaled and moved his lips against hers, as she traveled a slow journey across his. Tin's mouth caressed hers, his tongue parting her lips. Her tongue met his in a wicked dance, deepening and deepening.

Gripping her waist, he pulled her closer, and she could *feel* him, like she had that first night beneath his cloak. But this time, she wanted to continue to let him press into her. She yearned to explore what lay beneath all his layers. His heart beat hard against his chest, her hand, and that caused her to stop. Moments ago she'd hated him, and now what was she doing? Aunt Em would have told her she was being a trollop, and she wouldn't have cared. Dorothy was becoming too warm in places that needed to be touched, and she desperately wanted it to be by Tin's hand. But then she remembered they weren't alone in the house. Crow was in the other room—*her father*.

She pulled back as though she'd been scalded, peeling her legs from his waist. "That shows I forgive you, but it won't happen again."

"We both know it will," Tin rasped and tugged her to him.

In the morning Dorothy woke to an empty bed, remembering the kiss. *God, the kiss.* She would go on as though it hadn't happened, as if her lips still didn't tingle from it.

Voices came from outside her room—arguing.

"You think you can protect her?" Tin's voice boomed. "You didn't even stir when a clan of Wheelers rolled past last night."

"I would have woken up if they'd came in here," Crow spat.

Dorothy slipped on her shoes, grabbed her machete, and stumbled into the next room. Tin stood, gripping his axe while Crow's finger blades were out.

"Good morning," Crow said, retracting his blades and stepping toward her. "I was about to wake you so we could get started."

Dorothy bit her lip, not looking at Tin. "Crow, do you know what my real name is?" She didn't think she would ever call him "Father," because Crow was more comfortable, familiar.

Crow shook his head. "No, I didn't have time to learn it. Because of Locasta…"

"Locasta? What does she have to do with anything? Lion mentioned her name before he ran away, like the coward he is."

He rubbed a hand down the bottom portion of his face. "Just give me a moment. I said I would tell you, but this, this isn't going to be good."

With those words, he stepped outside, leaving Dorothy and

128

Tin exchanging a confused glance.

Dorothy opened the door and she and Tin followed Crow outside, then came to a halt. A gasp escaped her lips as she scanned the yellow brick road. It wasn't yellow any longer—the strip appeared as if it had been painted in crimson. Blood coated it. Fresh blood from the night before, but most was drying already from the heat of the morning sun.

As she scanned the area, there wasn't just blood, but bodies. Several male and female fae with large white wings and obsidian horns lay torn and broken with heads still attached. They looked as though they'd been beaten and run over with wheels. The Wheelers…

"They didn't take the heads this time." Crow sighed. "And it looks as though the males aren't safe anymore either."

"This is because of me, isn't it?" Dorothy said, wondering if something was going to abduct her right then. "We need to bury these bodies."

"I think you—"

"No, we're doing it," Dorothy interrupted Tin. She knew he was going to tell her to leave the South, and that wasn't something she could do.

She didn't meet Tin's gaze, even though she could feel him silently watching, brooding again. Because of her.

The night before he'd told her his true name, she'd kissed him, and then told him it could never happen again. And yet, she wanted to do it again, even while surrounded by blood. What kind of person did that make her?

CHAPTER SEVENTEEN

TIN

Just as Tin thought that the world had thrown him everything there was to throw, he found himself in a six-foot hole. Sweat rolled down his face and back. Dirt clung to the moisture and somehow managed to work its way through his hair to his scalp. He dug the rusted shovel into the ground and sat down to catch his breath.

Dorothy had better appreciate this. If he was going to work up this much of a sweat, there were a dozen other activities he could think of that would be more enjoyable than digging a mass grave. Not that he should be thinking about what had happened between them. She hadn't spoken a single word to him all day and *clearly* regretted kissing him. He couldn't say the same. In fact, he felt the exact opposite. What he wouldn't give to have her straddle him again, preferably with less clothing next time. He hardened at the thought.

"The grave won't dig itself," Crow called from above.

"Fuck you," Tin yelled back, his cock shriveling at the sound of the nuisance's voice. "If you're in such a rush, help."

"If only we could find more than one shovel."

Tin bared his teeth. "Use your fucking claws."

Crow flicked his wrist and the talons shot out. "They're not very useful when it comes to digging, but if it makes you feel better, I can demonstrate what they *are* good for."

Tin ripped the shovel from the ground and chucked it at Crow's face without getting up. "It's your turn."

"What a surprise," he said sarcastically, catching the wooden handle before it hit him in the face. "The Tin Man would rather pick up bits and pieces of dead fae than dig a hole."

Tin held his breath and motioned toward the ten-by-ten square Dorothy had marked out. It was nearly complete with just one corner to finish, but was already more than enough to bury what was left outside the abandoned house. "We both know this size hole is overkill."

"Fine." Crow disappeared from the opening.

The next thing Tin knew, a bloody arm came sailing toward him. He ducked to avoid being hit in the head. A leg followed, then a wet pile of organs squished to the ground, barely missing his boots. His breath hitched as anger swelled. "Damn it, Crow! What the fuck?"

"Hey!" Dorothy shouted. "What do you two think you're doing? These are *innocent fae* you're throwing around."

Well, they used to be. Tin winced—he was supposed to be working on his conscience—and grabbed a root to pull himself from the grave. By the time he emerged, Crow was silently, almost repentantly, carrying a torso.

Dorothy *tsked* when he let it fall into the hole. "No respect."

Tin wasn't going to speak his thoughts out loud. Telling Dorothy that they had already done more than enough for the murdered fae would only earn him further resentment. She felt guilty enough that the Wheelers killed them as they hunted for her. If this kept happening like he suspected it would, either he or Crow would have to speak up. There was no way he was doing

131

this again tomorrow. Dorothy would have to decide between reaching Glinda in time to stop Langwidere or burying half the population of Oz. Even Tin knew she would choose stopping Langwidere.

Crow continued placing body parts in the grave as gently as he could, and when he was finished, he begrudgingly took up the shovel again to complete the job. By the time everything was done, there was only an hour or two of sunlight left.

"We'll stay here another night," Tin announced, stretching his aching back. "No one would expect us to stay put after finding all that carnage."

Also he really, *really* needed to wash the day off and, though it wasn't exactly clean, there was a tub inside.

Dorothy nodded without looking at him. When she spoke, she directed it at Crow. "I'll run water for a bath. You both need it."

With narrowed eyes, Tin watched her walk back into the house. So she *was* paying attention to him.

"Tin," Crow said in a low voice.

Tin jerked his head to the side to find Crow much too close and eased back a step. "If this is about the bath, I'm going first."

"I need to tell Dorothy who her mother is. Just in case anything happens, she needs to know." He wrung his hands. "How do I tell her?"

Tin's brows shot up. "You're asking *me* for advice? Have you gone mad?"

"Pretend to be a decent male for a minute, would you?"

Tin bristled, but he was too tired to fight. He was also really damn curious about who Crow had knocked up all those years ago. Poor female... "Why not just tell her? Start with a name and how you met. Dorothy will ask a thousand questions after that and you won't have to worry about what to say. Just answer her."

"That's the problem." Crow grimaced. "Her mother is Reva."

Tin stared at Crow, the name processing as slow as molasses.

132

He couldn't mean... No. That was impossible. Dorothy's mother couldn't be the Wicked Witch of the West. There had to be some sort of mistake—a mix-up in Crow's memories. Maybe Oz had scrambled things around in his brain a bit when he broke the Curse of Unknowing.

Tin hadn't known much about Reva. He only knew that Reva was once the name of the Wicked Witch of the West, but she had put an end to anyone who dared use it. The name had faded from memory for most fae while she reigned because the Wicked Witch was so much more fitting.

"Reva," Tin repeated when he found his tongue again. "Of the West, Reva? That Dorothy killed? *That* Reva? Not some lonely barmaid with the same name?"

Crow's face contorted with pain. "So you see the problem then. If I tell Dorothy who her mother is, she'll have to live with the fact that she killed her."

Fuck.

"Fuck." Tin lightly scratched his head with his iron tipped gloves, loosening some of the dirt. This was going to gut Dorothy, even if her mother was a psychopath. "You're just as screwed as I am."

"Water's ready," came Dorothy's voice from inside.

Tin's whole body cringed at the mention of water—or as it was about to become known, the weapon she'd used to murder her mother. It almost made him want to skip bathing. *Almost.* It was more of a need than a want, and there was no way in hell he wanted to be there when Crow told her the truth. He bolted inside before Crow could try to trap him into assisting with their looming father-daughter conversation. It was the cowardly thing to do but Tin didn't give a shit. Dorothy already seemed to feel uncomfortable around him—being there to watch her break down wouldn't help any of them, despite his heart trying to tell him otherwise.

Once inside the dingy blue and yellow bathroom, Tin shucked his clothes off. Maybe he should've gone out to find a

133

river instead. He'd washed in them countless times since he was a young fae. That was before his stone-hearted coldness pushed all his childhood friends away, despite his best efforts. He should've known better than to say his friend's mother dying wasn't a big deal because everyone died. And he shouldn't have eaten an entire loaf of bread in front of near-starving toddlers. Tin had wanted to say and do the right things then—he'd watched everyone else in the village and copied their mannerisms—but he was never shown compassion. He couldn't understand when he needed to pretend and when he didn't. It became easier as he got older, but by then it was too late. It was only during those two years with his heart that he realized what sympathy really meant and how much the world lacked it.

Tin stood naked, staring at his pile of dirty clothes. After his bath, he would need to give them a good shake, but ridding himself of filth wouldn't be so easy. One day Dorothy would realize he wasn't good, and she would leave him. No amount of time could take away the blood already staining his hands.

With a heavy sigh, he ignored the film floating on the water and stepped into the tepid bath. The previous owners had thankfully left a bar of soap behind. Once the dust was blown away from the soap, it would clean him well enough.

A quiet knock came on the door. "Tin?"

He jerked upright, sloshing water over the edge of the tub. His heart pounded at the sweet sound of Dorothy's voice addressing him. It had only been less than a day since she'd spoken directly to Tin, but it felt like an eternity. "Yes?"

"Thank you," she whispered through the door. "For digging the grave."

He hesitated to reply because that gave her the chance to end the conversation, but he couldn't stay silent forever. "You're welcome."

"Dorothy?" Crow asked from farther away. He sounded dejected, even to Tin. "We should talk about your mother."

Tin immediately sunk under the water to avoid overhearing

the conversation, only allowing enough of his face to surface so he could breathe. He scrubbed his hair furiously until his scalp ached, then picked away the dirt that somehow made its way under his fingernails, despite the gloves. Soapy bubbles floated around him, mixing with the filth. Still, he washed a second time, and a third.

When a heart-wrenching cry—muffled by the water—hit his ears, Tin felt it as a blow to his chest. He sunk completely under and held his breath until his lungs ached. His heart thundered inside him, and he tried to make it stop.

Dorothy had killed her mother.

But only after her mother had tried to kill her.

Fuck, fuck, fuck!

CHAPTER EIGHTEEN

DOROTHY

"I need you to sit down, Dorothy," Crow said, clenching his teeth while his hands shook. "I'm going to tell you the story of your mother. I know you need to know who she is, especially now that you're here and in danger."

Dorothy's shoulders stiffened as she lowered herself on the couch beside Crow. She was nervous yet eager to hear the story of how Crow and her mother had met. And she wasn't alone anymore, like she'd been in Kansas. She had Crow and there was Tin, but now she also had someone who was a mother... She'd never had one of those before.

"I'm going to begin with you, Dorothy, and how you came about." Crow bit his lip and turned to face her. "I've been in love twice in my life. First with Locasta."

"Holy hell, is she my mother?" Dorothy had already heard not so good things about the Northern Witch.

"No!" he said hurriedly. "What I had with Locasta wasn't real, though. I fell in love with someone who didn't truly exist. Locasta pretended to be good, and like Langwidere, she wasn't."

Why was he talking about Langwidere? If she was the second person he was in love with, Dorothy would collapse right there.

"I know when you first came to Oz when you were younger, you were led to believe that the two good witches were from the North and the South," Crow continued. "That isn't true for one of them. Eventually, when I found out Locasta had secretly been murdering and plotting to rule territories, I went to the West to start warning people there. What I didn't expect to find was a certain female—one who was strong, challenging, and found my witty charm to be … charmless." He chuckled sadly and rubbed at his lower lip. "Yet somehow through our fights, our arguing, we fell in love with each other, even though we were completely opposite in every way. I loved her, truly loved her … I still do. Then you came along, and Locasta showed up at your birth. She'd been planning her actions for some time. We didn't know, yet we should have been prepared anyway. Locasta first cursed your mother, then took you into her arms. She told me she was turning you into a changeling before she cursed me to the cornfield—the place where you eventually found me—with a scrambled brain."

Dorothy covered her mouth, her breath coming out uneven. "Oh, Crow…"

"That's not all. When I got my memory back, I remembered *everything*, and I chose not to reveal certain things. I didn't go searching for you later because I knew you already had a family, and you would have been happier there without knowing the truth."

"That's not true." Dorothy wrapped her hand around Crow's. "Where is my mother now? Did you break her curse? Or do we still need to break it?"

"No, her curse was never broken." Crow inhaled sharply. "Her name was Reva."

Reva… Reva… Dorothy didn't know anyone by that name, but it sounded pretty. "I don't know her."

"Yes, you do. Locasta turned Reva into her plaything to

137

wreak havoc. She changed the way Reva looked, made her hideous so my last memory of her would be repulsive…" Crow closed his eyes, tears running down his cheeks. This was the first time she'd ever seen him cry, and her heart clamped up. "The Wicked Witch of the West once had a name—Reva."

Dorothy inhaled a ragged breath, unable to release it. Her entire body couldn't move. The Wicked Witch. Reva was the Wicked Witch. Reva was dead. Because of Dorothy. Dorothy had killed her. She'd killed her own mother. And Reva had been the love of Crow's life. A wounded sob escaped her lips as both hands came to cover her face, to try and stop the ugly feelings from pouring out.

Crow folded his arm around her but she wiggled out of his grasp and stood. "I did this to you. I killed her when I could have come up with another way."

"It wasn't your fault, Dorothy. It was Locasta's."

Locasta had taken Dorothy and swapped her out with another baby, so she would have never known. Not when she'd met Crow and he talked in riddles and strange sentences most of the time. "What about the human I was swapped with? Where is the real Dorothy now?"

"I don't know." He placed a hand to his chin and shook his head.

"You don't know?" She raised her voice then, because the real Dorothy deserved to go home, back when Aunt Em and Uncle Henry were still alive. But the second part was impossible. "I've been gone for ten years! Haven't you looked? Didn't you try?"

"Of course I did!" Crow exclaimed. "Do you think I'm Lion? I'm not a coward. I went straight to Locasta after you left. She only laughed in my face, broke my wings, and told me she'd found the perfect place for the girl. All she wanted was for me to be her lover again. I left then and continued searching, but came up with nothing."

Dorothy would have to eventually go searching for her, after

138

finding Langwidere.

"But..." Crow's brows lowered in confusion. "What I don't understand is how you managed to kill her with the water. It must've been the magic of the shoes combined with your power. You do have half of her, you know." He smiled, almost melancholic, as if he was recalling a memory. "Reva cared for the people of Oz. Before she was cursed, she wouldn't have done any of the terrible things she was forced to do. I know she didn't know what she was doing when she attacked you, attacked me—"

"I think I want to be alone for a little bit." Dorothy couldn't listen to any more of it. She'd killed her own mother who was actually *innocent*. Hot tears started to pour down her cheeks as she walked toward the front door.

"I understand," Crow said. "I'll give you some time to think over everything while I search for supplies to bring with us. I'll be back before the sun sets."

"All right," Dorothy whispered as they stepped outside.

"I love you. Deep down, even when my brain wasn't working properly, I knew you were my daughter." He wrapped his arms around her, but she couldn't bring herself to return the hug.

She watched as he walked away, slipping through the trees. As soon as she couldn't see the outline of Crow's—her father's—form, she released her tears fully.

After a while had passed, she gathered her courage and went back inside the house. The bedroom door was cracked, and the bathroom entrance stood wide open. She peered down at her filth and decided to get cleaned up, and possibly wash away how she felt.

As she stepped inside the mostly-clean bathroom, she took stock of the pale blue walls, the bright yellow floors, the tub already filled with fresh warm water. Tin. Tin had done that for her...

Dorothy couldn't think about him. She'd been trying not to all day. Even though she'd been avoiding him, she'd snuck glances his way earlier, too many to count. She couldn't help it.

Quietly, Dorothy stripped out of her clothes and stepped down into the water. Perhaps she could be all right about killing the Wicked Witch when she'd been wicked. *Reva.* The witch now had a name. But that wicked fae wasn't only her mother, she was Crow's true love, and she'd *murdered* her. Murdered the happiness that could have been. She sank her head into the depths of the water and cried once more. She watched as the bubbles floated to the surface, hoping Tin wouldn't be able to hear her. But she knew he had to have earlier.

When her tears were gone and she needed to breathe, she lifted upward and washed everything clean.

After she dried off and got dressed, Dorothy went out of the bathroom and stood in the middle of the house, unsure where to go. There was the living room and outside, but she didn't want to be alone again. Her gaze shifted to the cracked door leading to the bedroom. He'd left it open for her.

Dorothy chose to walk inside the bedroom. Mostly darkness spilled across the room because of the barricades. Tin lay on his side, bare-chested, facing the barriers of the window.

In case he was sleeping, she slowly got on the bed and curled her arms around his warm waist. "Thank you for the bath," she whispered.

He rolled over so he was facing her and draped his arm around her waist. "I'm the one who's supposed to be holding you."

"So you know…" She didn't meet his eyes. "You now know what happened to my mother and what a horrible person I am."

"Crow only told me your mother was Reva before he came to talk to you. Nothing else."

Dorothy needed it off her chest, out of her mouth, so she fed him the rest, the entirety of Crow's story. During it all, Tin's expression didn't change—he stayed watching her just the same.

"I'm horrible," she said when she finally finished.

"You're not horrible." Tin's arm tightened on her waist. "If

140

anyone is, I am. Look at all I've done."

Dorothy moved her hand to his beating heart. The thump-thump sang against her palm. "But you didn't have this at the time."

"I didn't have a beating heart before the Wizard either. And back then, never once did I swing my axe to kill." There was something in his voice that sounded like anguish, and she knew he regretted everything.

"Losing a heart after you've had one would make murderers and monsters out of any of us." There were times when she was going to lose the farm that she'd wanted to go out and commit murder herself. If she'd had a heart of stone, perhaps she would have followed through with it.

"I told you your heart was kind," he said, kissing her forehead.

Dorothy shifted closer and he turned so she could rest her head against his chest. She tried shutting her eyes and sleeping, but that was when the memories decided to creep back in.

"Look at you, just a little girl." The Wicked Witch laughed, shrill and high-pitched. "One who no one would ever want. You'll give me those slippers or I'll find a way to pull all your bones through your flesh and let my winged minions lick them clean. Then I'll wear your skin as gloves while slipping on the shoes."

Dorothy trembled while studying the witch's emerald green eyes, the color matching her skin. The witch's nose came to a sharp curled point and her brown hair hung to her waist in matted waves. She didn't know what to do. Her friends were outside trying to get in, but they couldn't.

Her gaze fell to the bucket of water beside her. It was given to her to drink, the remainder of the room empty of anything. The water was the only weapon that Dorothy could use to distract the witch and give herself a chance to run.

Not taking her eyes from the witch, Dorothy picked the bucket up and jolted her arms forward. The liquid collided with the witch's face. And before Dorothy could sprint away, her slippers lit up a bright silver, growing brighter and brighter, until the room was nothing but the glowing color.

141

The witch screamed, a scream that Dorothy would never forget. The screams became howls until there was silence. When the silver went out, the room was clear again, and all that was left was the witch's black dress in a heap on the floor. Somehow, Dorothy, along with the magical silver slippers, had destroyed the enemy.

The door flew open and there stood Tin, Crow, and Lion, who'd come to rescue her, but she'd already won.

"She's dead," Dorothy said. "I melted the Wicked Witch."

Dorothy couldn't sleep then, not when her heart was beating too fast, not when her mind wouldn't let her rest. Her eyes remained open.

"Are you all right?" Tin asked.

"No," she mumbled into his chest.

"Me neither." Tin lifted Dorothy's chin so that her eyes met his silver irises. He had a lot going on in his head, too—she knew that.

And she would do something about it.

Her lips crashed to his in a desperate, aching, needy kiss. His eyes widened in surprise for a moment before he relaxed and kissed her back, his soft lips drinking hers in. Tin had been right—this would happen again.

The kiss deepened and Tin rolled to his back, taking her with him. She didn't pause as she straddled him in the familiar position that she had grown to love. Beneath her, she could already feel him hard and ready. She slowly moved against him while tasting the flavors of his tongue. He groaned inside her mouth. Dorothy could have sworn she tasted the flavor of that sound, too.

This, *this* was taking her away from everything that had happened—Crow's story, the memories. And *this* was something she could focus on and not have to feel sorry about.

Despite the kissing being heavenly, she needed more. Dorothy's hands went to her chest and she unbuckled her overalls with a soft click, then let the flaps drop to her waist. Tin studied her in wonder, staying ever so still, as she then unbuttoned the front of her shirt and peeled it off along with her bra, exposing her breasts.

Tin's expression grew hungry—he leaned forward and placed his hands at her waist as he pressed his mouth to her nipple, sucking and flicking it with his tongue, all while moving her body back and forth against his hardness.

Dorothy couldn't control herself—she ran her hands down his chiseled chest to the tie of his pants to unfasten it. With determined fingertips, she untied the strings while he shimmied them off, freeing himself.

He was well endowed, so much bigger than the one she'd seen before. She wanted to touch it, to taste it, to have it inside her. Her center throbbed at the thought of it all. Dorothy didn't care if she was a trollop—she'd done much, much worse than lay with a man.

His lips caught hers again, his tongue prying them open before it plunged in and out of her mouth. She angled closer and firmly gripped his cock, stroking it, the tip moistening her hand.

"Take my overalls off already," she begged.

And he did. He took everything off her until she was just as bare as he was.

Dorothy's arms wrapped around Tin's neck as he pressed his hand between her legs, rubbing the spot that needed it, rubbing it so perfectly. Then he pushed two fingers inside her. "You're so wet," he rasped against her lips.

Before she could respond, Tin rolled her over to her back, kissing his way down the side of her neck, in between her collarbone, the center of her chest, and down, down to the place calling for him. Dorothy's first instinct was to close her legs, because no one had ever been there like that, seen her like this. But her nerves disintegrated into a million pieces when his tongue stroked, licked, and prodded in between her folds. She interlaced her fingers into his soft hair, arched her back and moaned in pleasure when she swore she saw a constellation of stars.

With a low chuckle, Tin kissed his way back up her flesh to her lips once more, his hand cradling her breast.

Dorothy didn't want him to stop there, so she ran her fingertips against his iron scar, absorbing the warmth. "Just get inside me." She'd never talked like this to anyone in her life, but with him, she felt braver.

"Are you sure?" His silver eyes mirrored what she wanted. "I know—"

"This is what I need right now."

"Me too." He leaned forward, the tip of his nose skating up the side of her neck as he murmured, "Have you ever been fucked?"

"Yes, I've been fucked," she whispered, running her nails down his spine. He shivered beneath her touch.

Tin lifted his head, his eyes locking with hers like before. "No, Dorothy, I don't think you have. Not in the way I'm thinking about."

The moment he spoke the words, she knew them to be true, especially after what he'd already done to her. "Then show me." The tip of his cock angled right near the place where it needed to be. "Please," she begged.

In answer, his hips rocked backward and he thrust forward, filling her the way she needed to be. She moaned as he continued to thrust, harder, faster. Her hands grabbed his buttocks, increasing the pace.

Neither one closed their eyes as they watched each other. He was fucking her and now she wanted to fuck him. Tightening her legs around his waist, she flipped him to his back and ground against him until the feeling started building and building. This time when the release took control of her body, creating planets and nebulas in the constellation, she shouted his name.

Tin grinned and returned her to her back. He deliciously plowed into her over and over until her name came out in a deep rumble from his lips. They were both a sweaty mess, and breathing the same heavy breaths, as he sank down on top of her. With a lazy smile, he held himself up by his elbows, looking at her. "Perhaps this is the first time *I've* actually been fucked."

Dorothy couldn't help but smile too as he adjusted himself beside her, both of them studying each other. Gently, he ran a hand down her cheek. "I told you to use me however you wished, and I meant that."

Did he... Oh God... Tin thought she had only done this to not have to think about things, as if she wouldn't have been with him otherwise. Hurriedly, she pressed her lips to his to show him that things between them had become more, even when she hadn't asked for it. She wrapped her arms around him because they both needed it. "Next time," she spoke softly into his hair, "it will be slow and beautiful, and I promise to make love to you like no one ever has. Because there will be a next time."

His arms folded around her, holding her tight. "There certainly will."

Dorothy could feel his length hard against her. "Already?" She giggled.

"For you, always." His lips went to the place right below her ear, kissing gently, making her body heat once more.

And for the rest of the night, neither's body would remain quiet.

CHAPTER NINETEEN

TIN

❦————————❦

Tin woke just as the sun began its ascent. The warm light leaking into the room made Dorothy appear like a goddess as she laid naked beneath the blanket, her hair tangled from his hands. He wanted to weave his fingers into it again, tug her head back, and wake her with a deep kiss, but they both needed a break after spending hours devouring each other.

A break and food. With a smile that wouldn't leave his face, Tin slipped from the room to see what Crow had found for supplies. Had he ever felt like this? He'd never smiled like this, even when his heart woke for the first time. His stomach growled and his thoughts turned back to finding breakfast. There would be no rationing today. He and Dorothy both needed to regain their strength, and it would be easier to find food now that Dorothy was fae. His smile widened as he realized that meant she had a long future ahead since she wasn't mortal.

If things like this kept growing between them, and they became more, did that mean Crow would be his family one day? He inhaled sharply at the idea and his wayward thoughts, unsure how to feel, and cut a glance to the couch where Crow slept the night before last. It was empty, the blanket Crow used still folded neatly. *Strange*, thought Tin. But then he realized the likely reason—of course Crow wouldn't want to listen to Tin fuck his daughter. He and Dorothy hadn't held back their moans, and the slam of the headboard against the wall had nearly broken the old frame. Half the forest probably heard Dorothy cry out his name. Multiple times. He grinned, pleased with himself. Crow was most likely passed out in his hammock just out of earshot.

Tin crept through the small abandoned house, looking for the supplies. Surely Crow wouldn't risk taking them with him when they would be safe here from scavenging animals. He stepped outside and scanned the immediate area.

"Crow?" he called as loudly as he dared. He didn't want to attract Wheelers, but if any did creep out of the shadows, he'd chop their heads off to send to Langwidere. None had traveled past the house last night. If they had, they would've stopped to investigate all the noise he and Dorothy had made. "It's safe to come in now." Not even the wind dared rustle the leaves. "This isn't the time to be petty."

When silence was his only response, Tin eased back inside the house without turning his back to the woods. This wasn't good. Crow wouldn't go so far out that he couldn't keep an eye on the house. He slid the bolt, locking the door. It wouldn't do much to keep out any real danger, but it would slow an enemy down.

Tin returned to the bedroom and shook Dorothy's bare shoulders gently. "Dorothy, wake up."

She groaned with a sheepish smile. "As much fun as last night was, I need sleep."

"I would love to let you, but that's not why you have to get up." He left the bedside and began collecting her clothes as worry gnawed at him like a wild beast. "Crow hasn't come back."

She bolted off the bed. "What do you mean?"

"Exactly what I said." He handed her the clothes and she

immediately slipped them on while he grabbed his axe from the floor.

"Maybe we scared him off?" She bit her lip, her face turning a deep shade of scarlet.

Tin shook his head. "I thought the same thing, but when I called for him outside, there was no reply. I have a bad feeling about this."

Dorothy met his gaze, her eyes wild. "Perhaps he didn't hear you. Perhaps he camped too far away. Or he could be sleeping very soundly like he did the other night. You two worked so hard burying the bodies and then he went for supplies... He had to be exhausted, so that's possible, right?"

Tin gently gripped her upper arms. "Breathe, Dearheart. We'll find him."

"But what if—"

Tin kissed her quickly, not out of passion but to silence her. "We will find your father, I promise. Stay calm and please, I'm begging you, listen to me. Can you do that?"

Dorothy, red-faced with worry, nodded.

He hoped she would this time—her track record with listening was abhorrent. "Good. Then take a deep breath."

Dorothy listened and Tin did the same. Once they had both exhaled, Tin collected one of her overall straps and buckled it over her shoulder. He made sure to use measured movements so as not to show how concerned he was. Having Dorothy panic would only make finding Crow harder and slow them down.

"There," he said when Dorothy was dressed and fitted with her machete. "Now we're going to search the woods for any sign of Crow or his belongings. Stay close to me and keep an eye out for his hammock."

Tin waited for Dorothy to nod before turning to lead the way. Her footsteps hurried behind him, barely noticeable over the echo of his pulse. If Crow was gone, the enemy knew where Dorothy was. Crow was the easier target between her protectors, especially if he had decided to camp outside. Now all Dorothy had was Tin, which would've normally been enough, but he was only one male. If an entire Wheeler clan came at them, if Lion had tagged along, or worse yet, Langwidere, there was no way he could win alone. Dorothy had a weapon now, but she wasn't trained in using it. Even her fae power was raw. She'd wielded it to escape Lion but that didn't mean she knew how to tap back into it.

Fuck.

As they walked, Tin shoved his iron-tipped gloves on and flexed his fingers. He was getting ahead of himself. Crow could've been eaten by a gremlin for all he knew which would've been a mercy compared to Langwidere. Just because something bad might have happened didn't mean Langwidere was behind it. But this was the South—a place that had become a land of blood and death because of her.

After ten minutes of searching with no luck, Dorothy grabbed Tin's arm. "I didn't say it back."

Tin paused. "I don't understand."

"To Crow," she clarified. "He told me he loved me before he left and I said nothing. I just let him walk away to gather supplies without telling him how I felt."

Tin's new organ cracked for her. "Dearheart," he whispered and used his knuckles to lift her chin. Her brown eyes glistened with unshed tears and her chin wobbled, but he refused to break their gaze. She had to know he meant what he was about to tell her. "Crow knows you love him. You didn't have to say a word. He understood that telling you about your mother would hurt and, I suspect, fully anticipated the reaction you gave him. Hell, he probably expected worse, but you're strong and brave and, most importantly, his daughter. Crow has known you loved him since you left for Kansas and he'll know you love him even if he goes another five hundred years without hearing the words from your lips."

Tears fell then, coating Dorothy's face. "I *have* to tell him."

"All right," Tin relented, drawing her in for a hug. "When we find him, you will, but for now, you have to continue to stay strong."

Dorothy sniffled against his chest before breaking away to wipe her face. "You're right. I'm sorry. We don't have time to waste on my crying when we could be finding clues."

Tin gave her a reassuring smile and turned his focus back to the search. It wasn't much longer before they ran across a fallen tree. Except, it hadn't *fallen* but had been cut down. Tin pushed Dorothy behind him and slowed his approach.

A piece of knotted rope was still tied near the top of the tree, just below the heaviest branches, with a small bit of ripped fabric clinging to the end. *Shit.* He already knew what he would find when he looked up, but he prayed Dorothy wouldn't follow his glance. There, dangling from a tree a few feet away, was the rest of Crow's hammock. On a lower branch, the overstuffed bag of supplies hung haphazardly, as if stuck there after falling. How Crow ever made it that high without being able to shift was a mystery.

"Tin…" Dorothy wheezed. "Look."

His eyes snapped to the ground where she pointed. Deep lines gouged the dirt. Dozens of them. And he knew, just as Dorothy seemed to know, that they came from the Wheelers. Tin studied the tree stump, taking in the sharp marks, and understood exactly what had happened. They had cut him down and took him. But where? Where were Lion and Langwidere?

"Damn it! Mother fucking Wheelers and their shit ass puppet master." Tin pressed the heels of his hands into his eyes. Their enemy was going to divide and conquer. Whatever it took to get Dorothy's head… Because, Tin realized with a start, *she* was the rightful heir to the West. He pinned her with a look. "*Fuck.*"

"The Wheelers have him," she said quietly. "Do you think he's still alive?"

"I don't know," Tin admitted. "But Dorothy, you're in more danger than I thought. If Langwidere knows who your mother is, she won't stop until she gets what she wants. Langwidere may

150

not rule here yet, but she rules the West."

And what she wanted was Dorothy's head. A dead heir was no threat to her power grab, and why not add to her macabre collection while she was at it?

"What does my mother have to—oh…" Her eyes widened. "She controlled the West and, as her daughter, that makes me the next ruler, doesn't it?"

"Yes." Tin dug his gloved hands into his hair. *Fuck* didn't even begin to cover it. "We have to find Crow before it's too late. Glinda will have to wait a little longer so we can follow these tracks while they're still fresh."

"Of course." She jumped over the tree, following the map of lines. "Do you think they came this way, or went that way?"

There was really no telling based on the tracks alone. If they had followed Crow from the house, which Tin suspected they had, the tracks would lead away from it. "That way," he said, nodding in front of them. "Let's get our supplies first."

Tin would never be able to salvage the hammock, so he left it tied above them and grabbed Crow's bag from the branch. With a quick glance, he checked the contents. Fruit—now bruised—and a moldy heel of bread. He threw that over his shoulder. A rope, two canteens, a wrinkled map, and a small assortment of daggers. He handed one of the weapons to Dorothy just to be on the safe side and tucked another one into his boot.

He rose from his crouched position, swung the bag over his shoulder, and leaned in to kiss Dorothy's head. For a moment, he closed his eyes and breathed in her scent to calm himself. He wouldn't ask her to stay behind because he knew she wouldn't, but if anything happened to her… He swallowed a snarl and planted another kiss on top of her head. They had to go now if they had any hope of intercepting the Wheelers before they reached Langwidere.

Lion would likely be there too, that backstabbing coward of a fae. This time Tin did snarl. Dorothy had lost many things in her life, but he sure as shit wasn't going to let her lose her father.

Tin stepped away and gave Dorothy's hand a quick squeeze. "Let's go save Crow."

CHAPTER TWENTY

DOROTHY

Dorothy and Tin had been trekking through the lush foliage, following the maps of lines, heading deeper down into the South. But she didn't know if they were even going in the right direction. The Wheelers could have taken Crow anywhere, or he could be dead...

The current line they followed looped around and ended back at the yellow brick road with no other path to follow except the road itself. Dorothy gripped the handle of her machete and walked closely next to Tin alongside the road.

There was no other sound enveloping them besides the light buzz of bugs singing.

"I suppose we'll just go the way we were originally following," Dorothy said, gnawing on the inside of her cheek. It was the same direction Lion had run off in, but where was he now? It was obvious that Langwidere was just as cowardly as him if she had to send Wheelers to do her dirty work.

"We'll monitor the dirt in case we see Wheeler tracks veering off and giving any more clues." Tin raised his axe over his shoulder, and together they continued their journey to hopefully find Crow alive.

As they walked farther and farther beneath the powerful rays of the sun, Dorothy couldn't help but wonder what if Crow really was dead. And if so, it would have been exactly like her mother—Dorothy's fault. She may not have killed him, but she might as well have because he'd gone out searching for supplies to give her space. Then he'd chosen to stay away to give her even more space. She'd been selfish, wasting time skin-to-skin with Tin. One of the happiest nights of her life had led to one of the worst mornings. She didn't want to regret it.

The soft tap of a finger came at the side of her head. "Stop thinking like that."

"Like what?" she huffed, moving Tin's finger from her temple.

"Negatively." Tin grasped her upper arm, causing her to stop, his silver eyes flashing into hers. "What happened to the Dorothy who was going to conquer everything? What happened to the Dorothy who locked me in a room and snuck away to do what she believed was right? That confident Dorothy."

Her shoulders slumped. "She's hiding. That Dorothy didn't know she was fae, that Dorothy didn't know she killed her own mother, that Dorothy didn't know she could be the reason her father might be dead, and that Dorothy didn't know there was a lunatic fae female collecting heads and wearing them for pleasure!"

"Well"—Tin leaned forward until his nose was touching hers, his breath warm against her lips—"let *that* Dorothy know that if she doesn't get her ass out of hiding, she won't win." Lifting his head slowly away from hers, he pulled something from behind his back and pushed a round piece of pinkened faerie fruit in front of her face. "Here. Eat."

Eating was the last thing Dorothy wanted to do at that moment, but she took the fruit from his palm. "Fine," she grumbled. He smirked and she tried not to smile as she pressed the fruit in between her teeth and bit in. The sweet juice spilled into her mouth, tasting like honey, and it was the only heavenly thing that had happened to her that day. It was better than any fruit she'd had back at home.

As they continued on their path, they ate in comfortable silence. She looked toward bright and colorful homes that appeared deserted. Like the other part of the South where Dorothy encountered the satyr, there were also grave markers, but too many for her to stick around and count.

The brick road curved down a sloping hill, then went up and dipped again, all while the sun beamed its burning rays against her skin. Up ahead, the trees seemed to grow closer, everything more wooded. A world of greens and browns and a dash of yellow. And still, no one in sight.

When they reached the top of the hill, Dorothy gasped. The yellow brick road was stained with splotches of dried blood. At least this didn't look fresh, but it couldn't have been that old, because the rain would have cleaned it away.

From the greenery to her left, a swish softly sounded. Dorothy paused, grabbing Tin's arms. His spine was already rigid, his axe raised. *Perhaps it was only the wind.*

With his axe, Tin crept forward and spread a red-berry bush apart. Dozens of flickering black and green bugs flew out.

Dorothy felt stupid, and she blew out a relieved breath.

"Come on," Tin said, returning his axe to its comfortable place over his shoulder.

She nodded, but her heart rate continued to spike as she scanned the area. Each step they took, the trees became even closer, until the sunlight could barely be seen through the overlapping limbs. Dorothy wished she had a lantern with her, but at least the sun wasn't eclipsed by the branches.

Dorothy stuck close to Tin—or perhaps he chose to be nearer to her. A rustle of branches came from above them, and she peered up, seeing nothing. With wheels for hands, she didn't think a Wheeler could climb up a trunk, but Lion or someone

155

else could.

Directly behind her a squeak filled the air, and Dorothy's heart froze in her chest. Hurling herself forward, she whirled around to find a looming shadow sliding out from behind a tree. A pale-faced female with matted hair lunged at her. Dorothy darted out of the way while Tin lunged toward the Wheeler with his axe.

"Don't kill her," Dorothy shouted, her eyes wide. "We can question her!"

Right as the blade of Tin's axe was about to strike the killing blow, he swiftly angled his weapon to the side. In less than a second, he had the Wheeler down on the ground with the wooden part of his axe against her filthy throat.

The Wheeler bucked and jerked, her wheels spinning at a ferocious speed, but Tin had her pinned down, holding her steady. As Dorothy shifted closer, she brought up her machete and held it to the Wheeler's heart, not knowing if she even had one.

Dorothy studied the female with dark hair, shining pink irises, and crimson lips sewn with white ribbon covered in dried blood. More dried blood mixed with grime coated her skin, making her appear animalistic. The Wheeler's face looked like that of a human girl, but her body was disproportionate, with a beastly curving spine and too-long legs and arms. At the ends of her appendages were spiked wheels where her hands and feet should have been.

Dorothy leaned forward, pressing the tip of her blade harder against the Wheeler's chest. "I'm going to cut the ribbon from your lips so you can speak."

The female violently shook her head, her body convulsing in an irrational manner. Did she want to have her lips sewn shut? Did she actually *like* having it that way?

"I've got her." Tin held the female tighter while Dorothy lifted her blade and easily sliced through the ribbon. At the female's throat rested a white collar with something etched in the center. Dorothy squinted and read the word, *Zo*.

"Zo?" Dorothy's brows furrowed as she focused on the female's pink irises. "Is that your name?"

The Wheeler hissed savagely, baring blackened and broken teeth.

"I wouldn't do that," Tin's voice boomed at the Wheeler. "Where's Crow?"

The female's gaze slowly shifted to Tin, her lips gradually parting as though she was finally going to speak. Instead, a deep, raspy laugh escaped her lips followed by another hiss before a wild giggle found its way from her throat.

Dorothy shook her head, scanning the trees for anyone else. These Wheelers were truly mad if they were all like this one.

Zo's laughter came to an end and her head shook side to side, not focusing on Dorothy or Tin. "Never tell," she whispered in a growl. Her head going faster and faster. "Never tell. Never tell. Never tell. Never—"

Tin picked Zo up and slammed her body back to the ground. "Where's Langwidere?"

Another round of laughter came from Zo. "Waiting for you at her palace." She giggled and roared with more crazed laughter, the pitch growing higher and higher. "Your head will be hers."

Before Dorothy could ask her another question, Tin raised his axe and swung it down across the Wheeler's throat, decapitating her. Blood rained upward, splashing Dorothy and Tin.

"What did you do that for?" Dorothy asked, incredulous, jerking her head in Tin's direction. "She was *talking*." Zo got what she deserved, but Dorothy wasn't finished.

"We have our answer." Tin straightened, using the Wheeler's tunic to wipe the blood from the blade of his axe.

Dorothy held both her hands up. "We still don't know where Crow is!"

"She said Langwidere was at her palace." Tin shrugged. "Crow and I should've known after seeing her old place that

157

that's where they would be headed."

"I still don't understand."

"They want Glinda's palace, her territory. That's why they're doing all this. And if so, Crow will be taken there."

Tin's words sank in. That made sense, and it was a better lead than anything they'd had thus far.

In the distance, the sound of squeaking filled the air. All the blood in Dorothy's veins stopped flowing as she looked further in the direction of the squeals. Tiny spots were heading their way.

"Oh no!" Dorothy whispered, praying and praying the Wheelers hadn't seen them.

"We have to hide," Tin said hurriedly, tugging her deeper into the woods. "Now!"

She grabbed hold of his hand and pulled him harder, her feet quickly moving over the dirt. While they dodged lifted tree roots, the squeaks grew nearer, more sinister. When the clanking of wheels and muffled howling reverberated across the foliage, Dorothy knew Zo's clan had discovered her body.

The Wheelers would never stop searching for them now.

Chapter Twenty-One

Tin

There was nowhere to hide.

The trees in this part of the woods had no branches low enough to climb, but even if they did, the Wheelers had somehow managed to cut Crow down. There were no caves, no buildings. Tin stopped running and spun, frantically taking in their surroundings. A few Wheelers, like he'd faced at Langwidere's, wouldn't be a problem, but it sounded as if at least fifty tracked them deeper into the forest.

Shit!

The loud screech of their wheels and the maniacal, muffled laughter surrounded Tin and Dorothy. It pressed around Tin's body, squeezing every ounce of rational thought to its breaking point. Dorothy would die if he didn't get her out of there. Hell, they both would.

He spun and took Dorothy's face in his hands, looking into her deep brown eyes. They were just as wild as he felt. "Run. I'll distract them."

"What?" She gripped his wrists to hold his hands in place.

159

"I'm not leaving you here to face those things alone."

"You will." He offered a weak smile—if this was the last time they saw each other, he didn't want her to see his fear. "Do it for me and for Crow."

"I can fight," she insisted, her grip on his wrists tightening.

Tin leaned in and kissed her. Her lips were warm and inviting, like what he thought home would feel like. Maybe that was what Dorothy could one day be. He put everything he had into it, willing his feelings into her for those few short moments, inhaling her very essence, then broke away. "If you run, there's still hope. Give me that. Give me a reason to keep fighting."

"I *won't* leave you," she said again.

The Wheelers were closing in. Flashes of movement in the distance caught his eye and he jerked his hands away from Dorothy's face. "Damn it, Dorothy!" He spun her around and shoved her in the direction of Glinda's palace. "*Run*. Go to Glinda and wait for me at her palace. If I don't come within a day, it will be up to you to save both me and Crow." *If Crow was still alive.*

That got her feet moving, but not nearly fast enough. She kept glancing back with uncertainty, pausing, and starting again. Tin growled and turned his back on her. If she wasn't far enough away from the Wheelers, he would be distracted. Distractions while fighting would only lead to his failure and none of them could afford that loss.

Tin took a deep breath, gripped his axe tightly, and ran toward danger. The screech of wheels became louder and louder until he couldn't hear his own thoughts. Individual shapes moved through the trees. Closer and closer. Tin inhaled and ran faster.

He trusted Dorothy to keep going, despite her track record of doing the opposite of what he said. She had promised to listen to find Crow, and this was part of that. Glinda would help her if Tin couldn't. As long as Dorothy was safe, he could do what had to be done.

Sooner than he'd expected, the enemy was upon him. But he was the Tin Man. This was what he was born to do: kill. Anything else he did was a conscious choice. His muscles coiled and his body slid flawlessly into a warrior's stance while his mind went completely silent. There was only an assassin and his prey. An axe and a target.

The first Wheeler fell with a single strike of Tin's axe through short, dark hair, and the second hit the ground without a head. Her pale face landed in a patch of mud with a squelch. He darted left, then right. Another Wheeler dead. The next dodged his killing blow and Tin's axe sliced through her arm instead. The dark-skinned female skidded across the forest floor, gushing blood.

That was the last easy swing Tin took. They were the leaders, faster than the rest of the pack, but the others were upon him then. Dozens descended at once. Their sharp wheels sliced his clothes. The kelpie scales held for a while, but even they weren't completely impenetrable.

While he swung his axe and dodged their attacks, a single well-placed blow tore into his calf. A pained roar ripped through the air and Tin attacked harder, dodged faster. He felt as if he were floating, his body moving while his mind watched. All of it instinct and years of honing his skill. But the Wheelers kept coming. More and more and *more*... Tin never suspected Langwidere had these many minions.

His breath became heavy, his movements sluggish. How long had he been under attack? At least thirty Wheelers had perished beneath his axe, but there were still twice that alive. Warm blood sprayed his face, blurring his vision, while more ran down the wooden handle of his weapon. Tin's grip slipped. His next swing came up short and landed in the back of a corpse as he stumbled to the ground.

Tin rolled to his back, bringing the weapon with him, in time to see a wheel slam down where his head had just been. He snarled at the female and lunged. The blade dug into her

161

sternum. Before the life left her bloodshot eyes, she head-butted him. He hadn't expected that—hadn't expected the Wheeler to have that much strength—and the strike sent him flying back.

An instant later, a wheel pressed up against his throat. He froze, waiting. All it would take was slight pressure for the metal to rip open his throat. He hoped he'd given Dorothy enough time to escape, that she was far enough away to avoid his fate and would soon be safe within Glinda's walls. He had to save Crow and rid the South of Langwidere and Lion, if only he could make it there.

Mostly, Tin prayed Dorothy would remember him well, despite the life he'd led.

He stared up at the Wheeler, refusing to die a coward with his eyes closed, when something hard slammed into his temple. The world ceased to exist.

Throbbing pain tore through Tin's head. He winced, rolling from his side to his back with a groan, and cracked his eyes open. It was too dark to see anything, but the air smelled of damp earth and rot. He reached for his cloak, but it was gone—left back at the house. Luckily he carried a few emergency supplies in his shirt pocket, and getting stuck in caves, while hunting will-o-wisps, taught him to always carry a source of light. It was a small mercy he still had the flat, oval disk on him. Resting it in his palm, he blew a quick breath over its surface to activate the magic.

White light glowed around him. It smelled like damp earth because it *was*. A large round tunnel surrounded him. Two deep gouges ran down the center of the floor where wheels had passed countless times. Tree roots hung down like curtains, swooping sideways to cling to the dirt on either side of the passageway in a web-like network.

Tucked into the roots, like decorations, were heads in varying stages of decay. There were skulls picked clean, some that still had milky eyes and rotting flesh, and others with so many maggots beneath the still-intact flesh that the skin moved. Selkies, urisks, merfolk—all types of fae alongside the much smaller heads of rodents and other forest creatures. A fresh ballybog head stared out at him in slack jawed horror.

"Well, fuck," Tin croaked. There was loyalty to one's master and then there was... Whatever this was. Obsession seemed an understatement. It was a miracle they hadn't added him to their collection, though he wasn't going to question it at the moment.

He needed to escape and get to Glinda's before Dorothy did anything rash. But how? Tin climbed slowly to his feet but had to hunch over to avoid scraping the ceiling. His head throbbed again, sparking light behind his eyes.

"Damn Wheelers," he hissed. His hand fell to his hip where his axe should've been, only to find it empty. "They'll regret not fucking killing me."

A soft caw came from the dark tunnel behind him. Tin spun and pointed the disk outward. In the center of the tunnel, hopping pitifully on one leg, the other tucked against his body, and both wings dangling uselessly, was a black bird with flickering brown eyes. It cawed again, a pathetic cry.

Tin's eyes widened in shock and his heart thudded heavily. "Fucking hell, Crow!"

The bird—Crow—let himself slump to the dirt. His sides expanded rapidly with his breath. Tin hurried to his side and knelt.

"What happened to you?"

Crow blinked slowly. Shifting took a lot of energy, or so Tin had heard, and it didn't seem as if his old companion had enough to shift back. Crow's agitated reply about shifting while they'd searched for Dorothy made sense now. Apparently, these weren't fresh injuries. Tin found himself almost pitying him, but shut down the feeling as soon as it began. Why would Crow shift if it put him at such a disadvantage? *Fucking idiot.*

"We have to get out of here." Tin grimaced. There was only

163

one option since he couldn't leave Crow behind. As gently as he could, Tin lifted Crow from the dirt. His bird form was nearly weightless. Brittle, thin bones poked against the skin beneath his smooth feathers, threatening to pop through, so Tin adjusted his fingers to press away from them. "Tell anyone about this, and I'll kill you."

A quiet caw came in reply.

Together, they navigated the tunnels slowly, pausing only when the distant squeak of wheels echoed. The tracks on the ground bent sharply at each turn, though some disappeared into soupy muck. Bones protruded from the dirt every so often. Tin recognized ribs and a partial spine, but he had no doubt there were more bodies stashed along the way—all the heads had to have come from somewhere. Where roots thinned, the Wheelers had carved out small den-like rooms with beds of sticks and hair matted to the ground. There was no way to tell how long they'd been down here or where *here* even was. The tunnels could span the entire south for all Tin knew. Maybe even farther.

Voices rose up somewhere close. A male spoke in low, hushed tones, piquing Tin's interest. The Wheelers couldn't speak with their lips tied, which meant they weren't the only ones to use these tunnels. If it wasn't the Wheelers, and it wasn't Langwidere, there was only one fae it could be.

"Lion," Tin rumbled. He set Crow down, tucking him carefully and safely into an empty nook within the tree roots, and stalked toward the voice.

Time to kill a coward.

CHAPTER TWENTY-TWO

DOROTHY

Dorothy hated herself, hated herself so much for leaving Tin. Why did she even listen to his self-sacrificing nonsense? She shouldn't have listened to him. It wasn't like she ever had before.

Tin was strong physically, and she knew that if anyone could take down all those Wheelers, he could. She'd tried to tap into the power that she supposedly had, but nothing came. Even now, as she ran across fallen leaves and patches of weeds, Dorothy couldn't call on anything. Perhaps she didn't truly have any magic. She didn't have power like her mother, nor could she shift like Crow.

Tears streamed down her face as she continued through the woods, only stopping for a few moments to drink water. As she came closer to the yellow brick road, all she could think about was how everything had gotten so much worse. Crow and Tin could both be dead, and now she was on her own again.

Dorothy stopped near a tree with several cobwebs hanging in its branches. Propping her back against the trunk, she caught her breath and tried to bring it back to a steady pace. The South needed to be saved more than anywhere else in Oz right now, and she desperately had to get to Glinda before Langwidere could invade her palace—if she hadn't already.

Gathering her strength for Tin and Crow, she pushed off the tree and continued. Even though she still didn't truly believe in herself, she needed to try, for her friends.

There wasn't time for her to stop, except to relieve herself, before night began to fall. She'd have to rest for the night, even though she didn't want to waste time.

Running alongside the yellow brick road was a town full of small homes shaped like mushrooms. Each one was a brilliant, neon color, some with polka dots, others with stripes. The town may have been beautifully decorated, but it looked just as deserted as everywhere else in the South. Yards were overtaken by weeds and dead flowers, and held clothing lines that appeared worn.

Dorothy stopped by a drinking well covered in gray stone along the bottom. She gulped down as much water as she could before striding up to one of the mushroom-shaped homes. This one was painted like a rainbow, and she wondered if there was a leprechaun inside based on its size. Gripping the handle, she twisted the knob—locked. She knocked a few times—no answer.

She was too tired to walk to any other homes so she shoved her machete through the glass beside the door, reached in, and unbolted it. The door slowly creaked open.

Quickly, Dorothy went inside, shut the door behind her, and locked it. A small sofa rested in a sitting room with an easel, canvas, and paint—some sort of art room. She collapsed on the couch, because her body was too heavy with exhaustion to do anything else.

As the silence enclosed over her, the tears decided to return, and she let them, because they were her only comfort as she fell asleep.

In the morning, Dorothy peeled her eyes open and focused on the dawn light spilling in through the window. Her gaze landed on a half-painted portrait of butterflies in a meadow. She hurried and sat up, remembering where she was, and that Tin and Crow were both gone.

Before she left, she decided to head into the kitchen to see if there was something worth salvaging to eat. Dorothy opened one of the doors and her body grew rigid. She shouldn't have been surprised.

In the center of the room, in the middle of the bed, lay two skeletons. A female in a violet dress, missing her head, and a male, completely whole, wearing a suit. Appetite gone, Dorothy quickly shut the door. One of Langwidere's minions must have taken the female's head and then by the look of things, the male possibly chose to end his life to stay with his lover in death.

She could barely breathe, and based on the couple's skeletons, even if there was food here, it wouldn't be good anymore.

Stumbling outside, Dorothy drank more water, then splashed her face with it to try and clear her head. She chose to pick a few pieces of fruit and nuts from the tree branches, and that would have to be good enough for now.

Carefully, she scanned the yellow brick road before crossing it. Once more, she stuck close to the trees.

The only sound in the woods was the soft humming of faerieflies. She didn't feel like getting stung today, so she stayed out of their swarming paths. During the night, she hadn't heard any Wheelers, but she wasn't sure if that was because there were none or if she'd slept through their squealing.

As she rounded a sharp curve, past white and lilac flowering trees, the palace came into view just ahead. Behind it, the looming ivory mountains rested. The building was larger than she could have ever imagined, with a steep sloping golden roof, and high magenta arches covered in bright yellow roses mounted along its trim. Dorothy couldn't help but smile as she crept closer and observed the pink glittering bricks—it was very like Glinda to have something so extravagant and colorful.

A pearlescent fence surrounded the entire palace, and the elaborately arched front gate was locked when she approached it. Where were the guards? *Shouldn't there be guards here?* She hoped she wasn't too late.

Dorothy gripped the bars and scaled her way up, gritting her teeth as she avoided the spikes at the top, before clambering down into the courtyard.

Brushing off her overalls, Dorothy surveyed the garden leading up to the entrance. Not a single space was without purple and blue pansies, except in the center. There, rising toward the skies, sat a shimmering light pink statue of Glinda, smiling.

Within the beauty, everything was quiet—most notably, no squeaks of any Wheelers. So perhaps Langwidere wasn't here yet—or maybe Glinda had already abandoned the territory like the other Southerners had.

The flowers brushed Dorothy's ankles as she trekked her way to the entrance. Large pillars connected to the front slope of the roof.

As she stepped to the porch, she expected to find the door locked, but it wasn't. She pulled it open, stepped inside the palace, and inhaled primrose. Dorothy would have expected it to smell of sugar, like Glinda herself.

The hallway was only a short length with more golden flowers in sconces hanging on a pale pink wall. As the foyer ended, Dorothy was met with a large open room, where a rectangular ornate golden carpet lay on the floor. Two chaises rested on one side of the room while four wooden chairs with white cushioning sat across from them. Along the back wall stood three sets of staircases, all leading upward to the next level.

Something wasn't right here, and Dorothy didn't hesitate as she brought her blade up. *Where is everyone?* In between the first two sets of stairs was another hall. As she approached it, a shadow peeked out from behind the staircase to her left.

A squeaking sound ripped across the floor as a Wheeler with dark raggedy hair charged forward. Dorothy didn't stop to think as she swung the machete—just as she would have if she'd been cleaving the corn stalks—and struck the Wheeler. He let out a muffled noise and toppled to the floor, blood spilling from his long arm. With swift precision, Dorothy brought the blade up and sliced through his neck with ease. She watched as the head plopped to the floor with a sickening thump. The body no longer jerked.

Dorothy gasped, and her eyes widened as she stared at the blood on her machete. She'd had it all this time but hadn't used it until right then. There wasn't an ounce of regret—none. And she would use it again if she needed to. She took one last look at the bloody ribbon stitched through the lips of the severed head as she passed it and continued down the hall.

Glancing side to side, she didn't see any sign of anyone else yet. What if Glinda hadn't left? What if she was still here—dead? Then what would Dorothy do? She couldn't think about that now.

Down the hall were open rooms, each unoccupied. At the very end of the corridor sat one closed door, and Dorothy's stomach sank with dread. Her heart thrummed in her chest and blood coursed through her veins as she followed the carpeted rug to the entrance.

Holding her breath and her weapon higher, Dorothy opened the door slowly with shaking hands. And she wished she hadn't. Inside were wooden cases, rows and rows of them. She covered her mouth to prevent herself from screaming, because they all contained heads. Blonde with milky skin, brunette with olive flesh, auburn with Grecian noses, pointed ears, some with curled horns—too many, all wide-eyed. Yet they were all perfect and beautiful—not an inch of rot to be seen. As her eyes continued to roam, they settled at the very end of the room, where a body wearing a pink glittery gown lay in a heap on the white marble floor.

Dorothy's hand clamped around her mouth as she hoped to God that Glinda's head was still attached. As she pressed closer, a relieved breath escaped her lips. Glinda was still whole, but she wasn't moving. Not a single twitch.

Jolting forward, Dorothy rushed to Glinda's side, feeling as though every eye in the room had followed her.

"Glinda!" Dorothy whisper-shouted as she picked up the good witch's limp wrist to check her pulse. "Glinda!"

Two emerald eyes slowly opened, focusing on Dorothy. "Who are you, young goose?" Glinda carefully sat up, her strawberry blonde curls bouncing beneath her flashy silver crown.

"It's me, Dorothy!" she exclaimed. "We need to get out of here."

"Ah, you've grown, haven't you?" Glinda lifted a hand and stroked Dorothy's pointed ears. "And become fae."

Dorothy didn't have time to answer those questions. "We'll talk about that later. What happened?" She clasped Glinda's hand and helped her to rise.

"It's Langwidere," Glinda said, stroking the high collar of her dress. It was the same gown she'd worn when Dorothy had met her. "I've been held prisoner in here for quite a while. She came in and took everything, leaving me without any power."

No power? This would make things even more difficult, but they could figure it out later. "I need your help. Crow and Tin have both most likely been taken by the Wheelers, Lion is a lying bastard who needs to be dead, and I'm fae as you've noticed. Everything is in shambles."

"There, there, my goose." Glinda folded her arms around Dorothy, holding her tight. A heavy scent of primrose invaded Dorothy's nose. Glinda had never smelled liked this—it was always sugar. Could someone's scent change? She supposed it could. Aunt Em's had over the years.

"Did you know you were a changeling this whole time?" Glinda whispered and pulled back with a giggle.

"No, I just found out." Dorothy noticed the expression on Glinda's face was no longer happy and giddy, but smug. She took a deep swallow and shifted backward.

"You're in luck because you can meet the human you were swapped with. She's right behind me." Glinda smiled wickedly and stepped to the side. Before Dorothy, within the glass cabinet, rested a female's head. It was a human girl with brown hair the color of Dorothy's—she looked exactly like Dorothy had in her human form except for a slightly smaller nose and thinner lips. "You are much, much prettier as a fae and will be able to replace the real Dorothy perfectly."

Dorothy couldn't speak, couldn't breathe, couldn't do anything but stare in horror at this monster. "You're not Glinda," she whispered. Dorothy's pulse accelerated as the room seemed to spin.

"Why, young goose, I have her same dress"—she swished the material side to side—"her same words, and even her same head. I *am* very much Glinda."

"You killed her?" Dorothy raised the machete, her entire body trembling.

"But of course I did. Since I'm wearing her head, I hold all her magic." Langwidere primped her curls as though she was getting ready for a ball, not talking about *murdering* innocents. "Don't get all dramatic and weepy either, because Oz wanted Glinda dead as much as anyone. He was even the one who sent Lion to ask me to steal her head for him. But I chose to keep it for myself."

As Dorothy lunged forward, a sharp pain struck her chest, ran down her arms and to her fingertips, causing her to drop her weapon. Her knees buckled and she collapsed to the floor, feeling nothing but stabbing agony traveling throughout her body. A quivering cry that she hated slipped from her mouth.

Langwidere unzipped the back of her dress and pulled it

down to reveal a white, silky skin-tight gown with a low v-neck, showing the curves of her breasts and a thin silver ring around her throat. *That must be where her head is attached.* She kicked Glinda's gown to the side. "That was a fun game to play with you. And for now, you will remain here until Lion arrives." Langwidere leaned forward and purred, "Then he will remove your head, and I'll wear it, along with your blood, as I fuck him for the rest of the night."

Dorothy was going to be sick. Even through the crushing pain, she tried to crawl forward to her blade, but Langwidere scooped it up. Then she stuck her hand into Dorothy's pocket and pulled out the small knife that Crow had collected and Tin had given her. Whatever magic the witch was using on Dorothy was too hard to fight.

"Thank you for bringing me these. Lion will enjoy using the machete when he arrives." Langwidere pivoted on her heels while Dorothy writhed in pain. The sound of a lock turning meant Dorothy was alone and trapped. But she realized with horror that she wasn't really by herself, because all the heads surrounding her seemed to be smiling.

Chapter Twenty-Three

Tin

Tin kept his steps light and soundless as he maneuvered through the tunnels toward Lion's voice. A dead Wheeler lay half-buried in mud and Tin stepped over its corpse. Farther down, a small furry animal bolted into a hiding place. His focus funneled, the heads lining the walls wholly ignored. It didn't matter that Tin's axe was gone—in fact, Tin preferred to take Lion out with his bare hands. His fingers flexed in anticipation. Strangulation was one of the most personal ways to kill, and this was nothing if not personal.

"My note was delivered?" Lion asked, his voice muffled. "Good. Langwidere will get to have a bit of fun with Dorothy before she collects her head. No one broke the order to leave her unbothered?" A short pause. "In that case, Dorothy should be arriving at Glinda's any time now." Another pause. "Stop fussing. I'll deal with our guests, but then I have to go remove Dorothy's head for Langwidere."

Tin fought to keep his breathing steady. They knew Dorothy was going to Glinda's and Lion seemed *pleased* by that. It was too late, then. Glinda must've fallen to Langwidere already, and Dorothy was walking straight to her doorstep.

Tin bolted forward in a blind panic. He made the next left toward Lion's voice in less than a second and found him alone with one Wheeler in a small circular room. Three other tunnels broke off behind the fae, but Tin barely noticed. He slammed into the male Wheeler, knocking him down, and broke his nose with the heel of his hand.

Lion jumped backward at the sudden commotion. His hair haloed his tan face with messy blonde waves, and his tail twitched nervously beside him. Faint light shining down from an opening hit Lion's bare chest. *An exit and Lion dead.* This kind of luck was uncommon. Tin grinned wickedly. The Wheeler struggled beneath him and Tin rammed his iron-tipped gloves into his throat without sparing him another look.

"Tin. You're awake." Lion spoke in a measured voice, but a slight waver gave him away. "I was on my way to see you."

"I'm sure you were," Tin said, standing. He took sideways steps to close the distance between them. "Crow as well. All your old friends defeated in a single day. How exciting that prospect must've been."

"We were never friends." Lion scowled. "Dorothy brought us together for a time, but we went our separate ways the moment we got what we wanted."

A flash of silver on Lion's hip caught Tin's eye. His axe. *That cowardly mother fucker.* He took a trophy before working up the courage to make the kill. "We all had our own lives to get back to."

"And look what you did with yours," Lion spat, now matching each of Tin's careful steps. "The fearsome Tin Man. The greatest assassin in all of Oz. Tell me, does the iron on your face still hurt as much as it did the day you received it? I watched the whole thing, you know. Your wretched screams were music to my ears."

Tin growled wordlessly. Much to his disdain, he had

174

screamed while Oz's men dripped liquid iron onto his face, but it was the last time he'd let pain in. Now he embraced it like a brother. Too bad Lion hadn't learned to do the same. "I would expect nothing less from someone who warms the bed of a monster."

"Oh, yes," Lion said with a leer. "I've warmed it many times over the years, and one of my favorite faces to fuck is the real Dorothy Gale. The sight of her lips around my cock, the way her eyes flutter when I make her climax—"

Tin pounced. His gloved fingers drove into Lion's bare skin, missing his throat by inches. Damn Lion's quick reflexes. Tin slammed his forehead into Lion's with a resounding *crack*. Lion fell back into the tree roots. Skulls tumbled to the floor around them and Tin winced as one nearly smashed his nose.

Lion took that brief moment to snag a mandible, still stuck on a root, and slammed it into the side of Tin's face. The pointed teeth tore into Tin's flesh. He could taste the blood on his tongue, feel it racing to his chin where it dripped to the floor. But he didn't give an inch. Because he *was* the Tin Man and would remain an assassin for as long as it took to protect Dorothy.

"Is that all you've got?" Blood sprayed from his mouth as he spoke, speckling Lion's face. Lion pressed himself into the wall of rotting heads as Tin leaned closer. He knew he looked crazed—he *felt* crazed—as he ripped his axe from Lion's belt. "This is mine."

"Tin," Lion begged, the word a whimper. "You know better than anyone what it's been like. The gifts Oz gave us—"

"No," Tin said in an unrelenting voice. "You *never* stopped being a coward."

Lion's lips parted to deny it, or maybe to beg again, but time was running out for Dorothy. Tin pressed the head of his axe into Lion's throat, pushing it slowly with both hands, while Lion clawed at his wounded face. The fight was over before it really began.

Tin loosened a shuddering breath as Lion's head tumbled to the ground, joined shortly by his body. Part of him wanted to drag the head to Glinda's to throw at Langwidere's feet before he killed her too. But if Dorothy was still alive, he didn't want her to see this. She had loved Lion once.

Leaving the coward where he fell, Tin hurried back to Crow. He'd managed to tangle himself in the root system in an attempt to get out of the nook that Tin had placed him in. "Where the hell were you going to go like this? Come on," he rasped, easing Crow carefully from the roots. "I sent Dorothy to Glinda's."

Crow cawed softly as if pleased Dorothy wasn't down there with them.

"Langwidere's already there," Tin added. "We have to hurry."

Crow struggled with his broken limbs, but Tin held him tightly against his side as he returned to the room with Lion's body.

"I won't apologize for killing him, but something tells me you don't want that."

Tin adjusted Crow slightly and, with his free hand, used the roots to pull them both from the tunnels. His muscles bulged as he supported his weight with one arm. The roots shifted beneath his boots as he tried to gather enough leverage to reach the exit. After a few tries, he found a solid foothold and shoved his upper body toward the sunlight.

Outside, the sun was high and warm. He'd parted with Dorothy in the late afternoon, which meant it had been nearly a full day he'd been underground, and it took less than that to reach Glinda's gates. Tin's heart rammed into his chest as he caught his bearings.

They weren't far from the yellow brick road—the entrance to the tunnels was at the base of a tree and resembled an animal den. He would never have noticed it, but they would need to keep an eye out now. If the Wheelers found Lion's body, they would report to Langwidere. Tin didn't have time to fight them off again, especially with Crow in bird form.

"Any chance you're going to shift back?" he asked. Crow struggled weakly until Tin set him down. Nothing happened for so long that Tin moved to pick him back up. "We're in a hurry, remember? If you can't shift back, I'll do this alone, but Dorothy would kill me if I left you behind, so just—"

A black cloud exploded with a *crack* and a few downy feathers floated through the air. When it dissipated, Crow was sprawled on his back, breathing heavily. "Go. Save. Dorothy." He was breathless and sweaty. "Now."

"Fuck you, Crow. It's not my fault you shifted when you shouldn't have. Get up and *help me* save her."

"I didn't mean to shift," he shouted. "But when you're suddenly free-falling from a tree, your body just reacts."

Not my body, he thought, because he knew how to control himself. The memory of how Dorothy drove him crazy all those nights hit him, unbidden. She hadn't even *done* anything to encourage his erections, but his body had rebelled. He bristled at the notion. "We don't have time for this."

"Have I mentioned how much I hate you?" Crow asked, dragging himself to his feet.

Tin rolled his eyes. "You and the rest of Oz."

"I don't approve of you and Dorothy." He narrowed his eyes. "She deserves—"

"Someone better? Kinder? More stable?" Tin laughed bitterly. He pressed a hand to his chest to feel the thump of his heartbeat, reassuring himself it was real. "Don't you think I know that? Dorothy deserves the world, but for whatever reason, right now, she wants me."

"Just because she brought your heart back to life doesn't mean she wants you."

The words hit Tin like a lightning rod. Crow was wrong; Dorothy wanted him just as much as he wanted her. "She's not going to be alive to want *anything* if you don't save the fatherly lecture for later."

"I can't believe you sent her to Glinda's on her own," Crow grumbled.

Tin strode down the yellow brick road before he could punch Crow. He was still too weak to withstand the blow Tin desperately wanted to give him. "Better than letting her end up in those tunnels with us, where she would've been hand-delivered to Langwidere," he shouted over his shoulder. "Now move your ass."

Chapter Twenty-Four

Dorothy

When the throbbing spasms shooting through Dorothy's body ceased, the first thing she tried to do was open the door. She kicked at the hard wood, then thrust her shoulder up against it. Nothing.

Her nerves were on fire and sweat coated her palms. The sick familiarity of this situation took her back to when she'd been all alone in that prison of a room. The one the Wicked Witch—her mother—had stashed her in. Only this time it was so much worse because she wasn't in an empty room, but surrounded by pristine, well-groomed heads with eyes that seemed to follow her wherever she stood. If she got out of this situation, she swore to herself she would light them all on fire.

In the middle of the floor, Dorothy sank down and cradled her legs against her chest, as though she was a child again. This time there wasn't even a bucket of water or magical silver slippers to aid her.

She kept her back to the head of the human she'd been a changeling for. Because if Dorothy hadn't been born, then the *real* Dorothy Gale would have still been alive and safe at home in Kansas. "It isn't my fault," she whispered. "That is all on Locasta and Langwidere."

The door clicked and Dorothy's head jerked up. She hurriedly got to the balls of her feet, prepared to barrel forward at whoever opened the door, when a wave of pain rushed through her veins. A choked cry escaped her throat as the door opened, revealing Langwidere in her silky ivory gown, the extravagant silver crown still resting neatly atop Glinda's golden curls.

"Don't try anything"—Langwidere smiled—"or I'll do that again."

Dorothy hated looking at that smile, those bright pearly teeth that had belonged to Glinda. "I thought Lion was coming to cut off my head," she spat.

"He's on his way." Langwidere yawned. "I grow impatient. Now, I want you to follow me into the sitting room. But if you try anything, you'll be down on the floor again, in worse pain than ever."

"All right." *For now.*

Grabbing the skirts of her dress, Langwidere sauntered her hips back and forth as the fabric dragged across the floor. Dorothy wanted to stomp on it and trip her.

Wondering if this was all a trick, Dorothy followed her down the corridor. All the doors that had been open were now shut. She would be obedient for the time, until she found the right opportunity where she could strike Langwidere without her throwing pricks of pain at her.

As Dorothy followed behind her, she asked, "Is your original head in one of those glass cases?"

"Only Lion knows how it was destroyed." Langwidere didn't even bother to turn around or glance at her.

Dorothy shouldn't have been surprised by this, but she still wondered how someone could easily toss aside a piece of themselves.

180

They entered the sitting room at the front of the palace. Langwidere arched her body seductively while stretching before she clapped her hands harshly. In answer, a loud squeaking of wheels came out from another hallway hidden behind the third set of stairs.

A female Wheeler, missing an eye and her hair shaved to the scalp, inched closer until she stopped at Langwidere's side.

"Where's Zo?" Langwidere asked, narrowing her eyes at the female.

The Wheeler shook her head and lifted a leg covered in sharp metal spikes.

Dorothy remembered Zo—she remembered Tin's axe coming down across the mad female's throat. "Who's Zo?"

Langwidere slowly sat down on the chaise, pushing her chest forward and crossing her legs leisurely. "My number one Wheeler."

Not number one anymore. But Dorothy kept her mouth shut, holding back a smile at her little secret.

"Sit," Langwidere demanded.

Dorothy sank down on the padded chair while Langwidere laid down like she didn't have a care in the world, as though she wasn't wearing someone else's head.

"Why all the heads?" Dorothy asked, glancing up at the vaulted ceiling and the glittery handrails along the staircases.

"You change clothes every day," Langwidere started, caressing the side of her face. "There's nothing different. It's all the same. I love my white dresses as much as I do my heads." She quickly sat up and leaned forward, studying Dorothy. "And I like your face, too. It's not quite as beautiful as your mother's, but close enough. If I could have had Reva's before she became monstrous, I would have taken it in an instant, but she was a tricky and powerful fae."

"You knew she was my mother?" Dorothy asked, trying to keep her talking.

"Of course I knew she was. Locasta and I have been working

together for a long time, but our civility had to come to an end sometime. After I gain your head, the West can never be taken from me, and I'll have all I need to conquer her territories and the Emerald City."

After Lion's last words about Locasta before running away, Dorothy should have realized that Langwidere had already known. She clasped her hands tightly together to keep her fingers from guarding her neck while desperately searching for a way to escape.

"Tora, bring me the blade!" Langwidere shouted and Dorothy stiffened.

The same Wheeler from earlier spun into the room with Dorothy's machete resting on her curving back. Langwidere's elegant hand curled around the handle of the blade. She rotated it in her palm, running her well-groomed fingers against the metal. Her demeanor appeared ravenous as she continued to silently rotate the blade while watching Dorothy.

There was nothing to attack Langwidere with. Her brain scrambled for a solution—*anything*. Dorothy's heart raced with too many emotions, her nerves flaring, her breath becoming uneven. Perhaps she could pick up the chair and throw it at her—no, too heavy.

"What are you thinking?" Langwidere asked slowly, toying with her lower lip.

"Nothing."

"When you lie, this happens."

A trickle of sharp aches, like spikes, struck at her flesh. Unable to hold back the cry, she screamed. It came again and again as Langwidere stood from the chaise with the blade, giving it a test swing. Tears pricked at Dorothy's eyes, and she couldn't even bring up her hands to swipe them away.

Langwidere inched closer—she was going to use the machete. Dorothy knew she was growing impatient waiting for Lion's return, and she wanted her head now.

Dorothy tightened her fists, her knuckles growing white. A

familiar wave of silver flashed before her eyes and she almost gasped. The rush came to her like it had with Lion, with Reva— she needed to grab at that speck of light. But the silvery hands within her passed right through it. A memory slipped its way out from a hidden place within her. Dorothy was a baby and a female with her face hidden behind damp brown locks of hair held her for a moment, whispering something at her ear. *Thelia.* Then a door had burst open and another female, with hair the color of obsidian, entered the room.

Thelia. That was part of Dorothy's true name. And the female holding her had to have been Reva. The silver grew wider, wider and she grasped it, holding tight. Her true name came to her then. Thelia Tunok Turolla.

"Did you not hear me?" Langwidere seethed. "I said to follow me upstairs."

Dorothy's gaze locked on to Langwidere's and she shook her head, her expression firm. "No."

"No?" Langwidere cocked her head and arched a blonde brow. "Then I'll make you come."

Pain slammed into Dorothy and she fell forward from the chair, dropping to her knees against the hard marble. *Thelia Tunok Turolla.* She repeated the name over and over in her head, fishing it forward to control herself, to make herself do something to fight back against Langwidere's power.

A heavy fog of silver flowed out from her, and a loud boom reverberated off the walls, shaking the entire palace. Dorothy's body vibrated in sync with it.

Langwidere stilled, her mask of indifference slipping to where Dorothy could read the fright before she put it back up. "Your magic won't save you. You don't know how to wield it yet, but I'll know how. Once I have your head." Holding the machete out, she lunged for Dorothy.

Dorothy closed her eyes, waiting for the blade to strike, but she felt something burst out from her. She opened her lids, finding Langwidere on the floor, propping herself up with her elbows. Dorothy's magic must have thrown her back, like it had with Lion. Beneath Dorothy's feet, the ground rumbled, then the marble started to crack and split apart.

Small pricks floated across her skin—Langwidere was using her magic, but Dorothy could barely feel it. Dorothy thought about her name once more, and this time the silver fog filling the room turned into a heavy cloud of smoke. She couldn't see anything, but she heard Langwidere screaming and screaming.

Then silence, the cloudiness slowly fading.

As the smoke cleared, Dorothy spotted the machete on the floor and snapped it up. A few feet from her, Langwidere lay on the marble squirming, convulsing. Dark veins, almost black, pulsed against her too-pale skin. Dorothy rushed forward and slammed her fist into Langwidere's face—*Glinda's* face. Her head must have been loose from when she'd hit the floor because it popped off, revealing a metal disc. But the body was still *moving*. Drawing her arms up, Dorothy plunged the machete into Langwidere's chest, puncturing straight through the witch's evil heart. This time, nothing was left twitching as silver continued to pour around them.

Dorothy's magic wouldn't stop. The silver poured out of her more and more until she thought she was going to burst, and she didn't know how to shut it off. Was it possible to die from your own magic? Dorothy's knees buckled, and she sank to the floor, her body growing weaker and weaker.

After several long moments of lying there in nothingness, the room started to clear again. Two warm hands lifted Dorothy's head up slightly, and she didn't have the strength to stop it from being taken from her body to one of Langwidere's cabinets. Gently, fingers brushed the hair from Dorothy's forehead, like she was a child.

With all she had left, she tilted her head back to look into the two eyes that were going to murder her, where death awaited. Above her was an unfamiliar female fae's face. Pale skin, chestnut-colored hair, and emerald eyes that were mirrors of

Glinda's.

"Thelia," the fae whispered, sadly smiling.

Another form crept forward with bright blue eyes and blonde hair cascading down to her waist. Dorothy jerked but stopped when she realized neither were Langwidere.

"It's okay," the emerald-eyed fae said. "This is Ozma. You saved us both from a lifetime of nightmares."

"What do you mean?" Dorothy's breath was coming back, her body becoming less exhausted.

The fae sighed. "Ozma is the rightful ruler of Oz, but the Wizard hid her away before he stole her position by using the silver slippers. She needs to go home and reclaim it to correct all that has happened. I, on the other hand, have a journey of my own to make. To visit Locasta."

Oz again? The slippers were still intact after all? *He* had them? Langwidere had mentioned how he'd wanted Glinda's head. Another person Dorothy had once believed in, who needed to die. Then she focused on the fae's last word. Locasta. Was this fae going to go there to wreak havoc with her?

Dorothy narrowed her eyes. "Who are you?"

"I'm Reva." She smiled. "Your mother."

Inhaling sharply, Dorothy sat up and spun around. "No, I killed you. The water, the silver shoes, my-my magic—melted you. You looked nothing like this." She recalled the green skin, the long, pointed nose, the gangly arms, and curving spine.

"No, Thelia, you didn't kill me." She paused, her lower lip trembling as she clutched her thin black dress covered in holes. "You saved me from the curse but somehow banished me into darkness with your magic. And now, your power returned me here."

"So I had you trapped somewhere?" Dorothy asked, horrified.

Reva nodded. "Yes, but at least I met a friend there when Oz pushed her into darkness, too." She looked to Ozma. "We helped each other survive."

185

Ozma wore a sleeveless light blue dress with rips and holes. Her voice came out strong, regardless of what she'd gone through. "Oz wasn't the only one who did this to me. A witch named Mombi did a lot worse." She turned away from Dorothy, and at the center of her bare back was a hardened patch of skin. "Mombi cut off my wings and butchered them until they were shreds of nothing." Ozma looked as though she wanted to cry, but she didn't.

Reva peered down at Langwidere's dead body, her hand covering her mouth.

"Langwidere killed Glinda and was wearing her head, and she planned on taking mine, too," Dorothy said.

The doors burst open and Dorothy and Reva hurried to their feet. Dorothy was ready for whatever was coming their way, but her arms fell back to her sides when she saw that it was Tin and Crow, both covered in grime and blood.

She didn't care how filthy he was—she ran toward Tin and threw her arms around him, inhaling his scent. "You two are late saving me again." Dorothy thought about the last time they'd come through the door right after she'd melted the Wicked Witch—Reva. *Reva.*

Dorothy released Tin and whirled around to find Crow staring at Reva, his lips parted.

Reva wore a neutral expression as her gaze held his. "I'm going to go to Glinda's room for the night and mourn my sister."

Her sister? "We need to see if there are Wheelers anywhere in here first," Dorothy said. Reva just came back, and Dorothy didn't want her mutilated by those monsters before she got to have a full conversation with her.

"I wouldn't worry about them. With their master dead, they'll be long gone soon enough."

Reva wrapped her arm around Dorothy's shoulders and kissed her forehead. "I'm sorry I didn't get to know you sooner." She turned around for the stairs.

"Reva!" Crow's voice sounded desperate, anxious, happy.

Reva's shoulders stiffened and she slowly turned around. The way she was observing Crow wasn't the sweet adoring way she'd looked at Dorothy—it was something furious and Dorothy wanted to shrink into herself, even though the anger wasn't focused at her.

"Don't you dare speak to me!" Reva seethed. "Don't you dare ever speak to me again. This, *this* is all your fault, and *you* are nothing to me." With those words, she spun around and hurried up the stairs.

Dorothy looked between Ozma, Tin, and Crow, the tension in the room heavy.

"Let me go talk to her," Ozma said, studying Crow. "For what it's worth, I don't believe it was your fault." Then she turned and ran up the stairs barefoot after Reva.

"Who the fuck was that?" Tin asked, clearly confused.

"Her name's Ozma, and she was trapped with Reva. She's the true ruler of Oz."

Tin frowned. "I've never heard of her."

It seemed as if no one had.

"I'm glad you're safe"—Crow cleared his throat—"but I think I'll search the premises and make sure they're clear." He pulled Dorothy into a quick hug. His eyes were glassy when he released her, and she knew that it wasn't because of her.

CHAPTER TWENTY-FIVE

TIN

Glinda was dead, but her magic was still present in the palace. Flowers glimmered and, in the kitchen, food miraculously prepared itself. Candles flickered to life when the sun began to set. Tin wondered if there was anything in the palace Glinda *hadn't* enchanted, especially when he stood beside Dorothy in the bathroom.

Pearlescent bubbles floated through the air. They drifted off the top of a large in-ground tub, big enough for half a dozen people, and released different floral scents when they popped. One landed on his nose. He shook his head in surprise and swiped it off, leaving his face and hand smelling like daffodils. His lips curled in annoyance.

"You should get in," he said, wiping his palm on his pants.

Dorothy poked at the bubbles, mesmerized. "Why don't you go first?"

Tin placed his axe on the tiled floor and scooped Dorothy up over his shoulder. She gasped and grabbed at the back of his shirt as he stepped into the waist-deep water. Dorothy's laughter bounced through the room. Tin let out a low rumbling chuckle as he set her down before him, the front of her body sliding against his.

"You should take that off." Dorothy splashed at Tin's shirt.

Tin obeyed, pulling the wet material over his head, and advanced on her. "So should you," he growled playfully, and unbuttoned her overalls before she realized what he was doing.

Dorothy's deep brown eyes held his silver ones as she loosened the buttons of her shirt and tossed it aside. Tin stepped back to admire her body and worked the ties on his pants beneath the water. It wasn't easy peeling the soaking material off, but he had a slightly better time than Dorothy.

When she slipped backward during the struggle, she emerged a moment later with her hair full of bubbles. "Help?" she sputtered.

Tin laughed quietly and searched out her foot, prying the clingy pants of her overalls away. "There. Now we can bathe."

Dorothy reached over to where an assortment of soaps and oils were arranged and began smelling each one. Tin waited patiently while she chose, but once she had, he plucked it from her hands. "What are you doing?"

"Washing you," he said as if it were obvious. "Turn around."

She turned slowly, keeping an eye on him as he poured the purple liquid into his palms and rubbed it into a lather.

"Lift your hair."

She collected the wet locks. "You know, I can do this myself."

"What fun would that be, Dearheart?" Tin brushed a finger down the back of her neck and rubbed the soap over her skin. She sighed as his calloused hands caressed her back, her arms, across her stomach, and over her breasts. The sound lit a fire in Tin's stomach. He wanted her—he *always* wanted her—but first they needed to wash the horrors of the day off.

When he was finished, he quickly dunked his head underwater in an attempt to clear away all the dirty thoughts.

There would be time for that later, he reminded himself again and again. He quickly scrubbed his body with the soapy water. Five minutes from now was *later*.

"Now you," Dorothy instructed the moment he resurfaced. *Later, later, later.*

"Just the hair," he hedged. Dorothy opened her mouth but he silenced her with his thumb against her lips, tilting her chin up. He wanted her but he also wanted this tender moment. "Just the hair."

"Fine," she relented, rolling her eyes at him.

Tin sunk down so she could reach his head. His eyes drifted shut at the feel of Dorothy's fingers massaging the soap from his hair. She worked around the bits of blackened bone holding one side of his hair back and fanned the ends out to float on the bubbly surface.

All too soon, her warm breath tickled his ear. "I think I've gotten it all out."

"No." Tin reached up and gently held her hands to his head. "I think there's still a bit left. Keep going."

Dorothy laughed, the sound bringing a smile to Tin's face. "I'm going to rub you bald if I keep going." Her fingers resumed stroking his silver locks.

Tin closed his eyes again to revel in their peace a little longer. Soon, it would pop just like the bubbles. Langwidere was dead, Wheelers now ran loose through the South, and Reva was back with the true ruler of Oz. No one had talked about the emotional ramifications of what transpired or what would happen next. Because no one really knew, least of all Tin.

"Are you sure we shouldn't be helping Crow bury the heads right now?" Dorothy asked.

"He wants to be left alone," Tin assured her. Who could blame him? The love of his life had returned from the dead and seemed to loathe him with a passion. Reva and Ozma had barricaded themselves in a room and refused to see anyone— not that anyone but Crow had tried. "How do you feel about your mother?"

"I'm not sure yet," she admitted carefully. "I still don't understand what I did to bring her back. Langwidere was about to take my head and my power reacted to save me. I thought I was dreaming for a second when she told me who she was. I ... need to talk to her but I think tomorrow will be a better day to start."

Tin took one of Dorothy's hands and brought it to his mouth, kissing her palm. "That's probably for the best. It's been a hard day for all of us."

"It has," she admitted, her voice still downcast.

He hated to bring her mood down even more, but there was still something he hadn't told her. He'd already explained how the Wheelers took him into their tunnels and that's where he found Crow, but he'd left out details. The heads, Crow's broken body when he shifted ... and Lion. He sighed. Better to get it over with.

"Dorothy." He sat up and turned around to face her. Water lapped against his abs with the sudden movement, and he forced himself not to stare at where her breasts disappeared beneath the layer of bubbles. "I need to tell you something."

All expression fell from her face, and she seemed to brace herself for more bad news. "What is it?"

Tin took a deep breath. "Lion was in the tunnels."

"Oh?" Something between fear and fury flashed through her eyes. "Where is he now?"

Shit. He almost didn't want to answer her. Yes, Lion was the enemy. He had planned to kill Dorothy and had hired Tin to deliver her so Langwidere could wear her head to conquer Oz. But once, long ago, she'd considered Lion a close friend. It was ... complicated. *Everything* was complicated now that he had his beating heart back.

"Dead," he whispered without meeting her eyes. "I killed him."

For a few moments, the faint pop of bubbles was the only

191

sound in the bathroom. Then Dorothy placed a hand on the unblemished side of Tin's face and ran her thumb along his cheekbone. "Good."

Tin looked at her to see if she really meant it and found steely resolve on her face. "Are you sure?"

"Of course I'm sure." She slid closer. "He wasn't the Lion I knew anymore. *That* lion has been dead for a long time."

Tin loosened a breath. He knew deep down that Lion's death pained her on some level, but what choice had he been given? If he had to choose between someone—*anyone*—and Dorothy, she would win every time. Besides, fuck that bastard. Lion deserved to die a worse death than Tin had given him.

"Let's get out of the water before I turn into a prune any more than I already have," Dorothy suggested.

Tin wasn't sure what a prune was, but he definitely didn't want Dorothy to turn into anything. He lifted himself from the tub and grabbed an oversized towel from the counter, holding it out for her to step into.

"Watch out, Tin. You'll turn into a real gentleman if you're not careful." Dorothy grinned and hurried into its warmth.

"Bite your tongue." He rubbed his hands over the towel, drying her body beneath it, and his cock twitched.

Dorothy stuck her tongue out at his teasing remark and he leaned forward, capturing it in his mouth. His tongue traced over hers in a dance and he tugged the corner of the towel so the front opened and she was naked against him. Her lips were warm and soft beneath his as he pulled her close, deepening the kiss. Dorothy leaned up on her toes to better meet him.

Tin pulled away and Dorothy whined. But then his lips kissed down her neck and across her collarbone. He flicked his tongue over the edge of her earlobe at the same time he released the towel so he could grab her ass. At her gasp, he moved back to kissing her throat.

Dorothy tilted into him, her pulse pounding beneath his lips. "Do you remember what I said before?"

"Can you be more specific?" he murmured.

A slight blush colored Dorothy's face. "I promised to make love to you like no one ever has, and I want to now."

Tin's breath caught. She had no idea how much he wanted that too. *Desperately.*

"Not here," she panted against him. "I want you in bed."

"Your wish is my command." He tightened his grip on her ass and lifted her so her legs wrapped around his waist. "You're not cold, are you?"

Dorothy ran her mouth down the side of his neck. "I'm sure you'll keep me warm enough."

Oh, he would. Tin practically barged into the bedroom and set her in the center of the bed. Despite the throbbing of his cock, he leaned back on his knees to look at her splayed before him. Her nipples pebbled beneath his stare and the moisture coating her center had nothing to do with the bath. It was for him—because she wanted *him.*

"Hurry up," she urged.

Tin laughed. "You promised me *slow.*"

"Not glacial," she replied with an amused huff.

He closed the distance between them and took her face in his hands. His lips molded against hers, lingering, exploring. Her tongue swept over his. *Slowly.* He smiled against her mouth and hovered over her naked form. Breaking their kiss, he brushed the hair from her forehead. His silver eyes swept over her features. "You're so beautiful."

One of Dorothy's legs wrapped around his thigh and urged him closer. "So are you."

"I've never done this before," he admitted, and Dorothy raised her brows at him. He chuckled. "Fucked, yes, but not … this."

"Neither have I. Not really." She leaned up on her elbows and set her forehead against his. "I think it's time for us to change that. Now."

"So impatient," Tin murmured. But so was he.

Their mouths met again, moving in perfect sync, and Tin pressed against her opening. His lips traveled over her jaw and down her neck, savoring the moment. When he ventured back to her lips again, he eased inside her.

Dorothy moaned and wrapped her arms around his neck, tangling her fingers in his hair. His movements were unhurried. Each tender thrust let him feel every inch of her as her hands slid over every inch of him. They learned each other's bodies for what felt like hours, switching positions and getting to know what the other liked. It was a long, exquisite torment as Tin held back, drawing out Dorothy's pleasure. When she cried his name, her body vibrating as she came around his cock, he spilled into her with a deep groan.

Tin rested his head on Dorothy's shoulder and fought to catch his breath. "I didn't know it could be like that."

Dorothy let out a satisfied *hmm*, apparently still unable to speak properly.

"I want to do it again," he said. Dorothy made a surprised sound beneath him and he quickly added, "later."

"Sleep first?" she breathed.

"Food first, then sleep." Tin kissed her damp skin. "*Then* again. In the tub next time."

She laughed and gave him a gentle shove off her. Tin rolled to his side. With a contented sigh, she snuggled into the crook of his arm. "Sleep first."

Tin pulled her closer and tugged the blanket over them both. If she wanted sleep, she would have it. He would give her the world if she asked it of him, though he knew she never would because Dorothy's heart was good. Much better than his. It was a miracle that she didn't care his was stained black around the edges—that it was beating again seemed enough.

He hugged Dorothy to him as his chest expanded. "I think I love you, Dorothy Gale." It may have been too soon to say it, but his heart felt it anyway.

She kissed his lips, then leaned her mouth closer to his ear.

"I have a secret meant only for you. My name isn't Dorothy. That name never belonged to me. It's Thelia Tunok Turolla, and I'm giving that to you because I'm falling in love with you, too."

Tin froze. Her true name—she trusted him with her *true name*. And, just like that, his heart swelled until he thought it would burst from his chest. "My axe is yours, Thelia. My axe, my life, and my heart."

"I promise to take care of them," she replied with tears glistening in her eyes. "Always."

Epilogue

Thelia

"Thelia," she whispered. The name felt natural. As soon as she'd discovered her true name, it suited her more than Dorothy ever could. Then, when she'd heard it roll off Tin's tongue, she knew it was there to stay. The night before with Tin was different—it was the start of something more than she could have imagined. Even though the Land of Oz wasn't done being mended. The South and West may be free now, but Locasta still ruled the North and the East while Oz still reigned over all.

She studied each of the empty glass cases. No more heads.

Footsteps entered the room and she whirled around to find Crow carrying something in his hand. "You need to eat." He handed Thelia a pastry covered in heavy white icing and colorful sprinkles.

"Thank you for taking care of everything around here," she said, accepting the warm dessert from him. "I told you I would have helped." He'd spent the rest of the day digging up dirt, burying every single head, including Glinda's. No one knew what Langwidere or Lion had done with her body, but at least she could rest in peace now.

"I wanted to do it alone." He quickly changed the subject before she could question him further. "Where's Tin?"

"Still sleeping." Tin had been resting on his stomach with her arm draped around him when she'd woken. She'd covered him with a blanket and let him rest because it was the first time she'd ever seen Tin appear so at peace.

"I still don't approve." Crow lowered his brows, sweeping his gaze across the empty cabinets.

"Why?" She tilted her head to one side. "Because he's murdered? We all have."

"No, I don't care about that." His lips tilted up. "It's because you're my daughter. But if someone has to be good enough, I suppose he'll do."

Thelia fought a grin. "You like him."

"Now, let's not be hasty here." He chuckled.

Bringing the pastry to her lips, she took a bite of the delicious sweetness. "So … have you talked to her yet?" She'd seen Reva's anger, but now that her mother had had time to sit and really think about things, perhaps she'd calmed down a bit.

"No…"

"Go knock on her door!" Thelia exclaimed. "What are you waiting for?"

"To be clear, I haven't talked to her. But I have knocked on her door. Three times."

Thelia folded her arms across her chest. "Tin would have broken down the door."

"Sorry, I don't carry around axes." He fought back a smile.

"Ah, but you do have metal claws that can extend. Perhaps try those next time." Thelia took another bite of the pastry. "I'm going to go talk to her."

Crow wrapped his arms around her. "Even if I don't have her, I have you, and that's enough for me." He was lying and she knew it.

"I really am glad you're my father, and I'm sorry I didn't tell you that before…"

"I know. We'll talk more later." He paused. "Now, go to Reva. I know she'd be happy to see you."

With a smile, she nodded before leaving the room to head to the stairs. After all these years, Crow was still in love with her mother. Her chest tightened thinking about the things that had been done to them.

As she grabbed the stair rail, she observed the sitting room. All the blood had been cleaned—Crow had done that too, and she knew it wasn't for his own benefit, but for her and Reva. The fracturing in the floor, and up the walls and ceiling, was barely visible. Only a hairline crack lingered. Somehow the magic inside the palace walls had mended itself.

Thelia climbed to the top floor and could tell right away which door had belonged to Glinda. Her door was the only one bright pink in color with silver flowers painted down its entire length.

Her heart beat quickly—she was going to see her mother again. Would it be strange? Would it be awkward? Raising her hand to the door, she softly knocked. "It's me, Thelia."

In a matter of seconds the door swung open, and Reva stood there with a smile. She was no longer dressed in a black cloth covered in holes. Instead, she wore a sparkling pink dress that was tight on top, accompanied with a poofy skirt, falling to her ankles. The sleeves were sheer with cloth cuffs at her wrists. Her hair, the color matching Thelia's own, was no longer a rat's nest but fell to her waist in a long, silky sheet.

"Come in." Reva waved her through the door, then looked down at herself. "This isn't something I'd ever wear. I prefer black. But my choices were limited—white or pink gowns."

Thelia thought about Glinda, and she tried not to let her eyes fill up with tears again. Glinda was not only Reva's sister, but had been Thelia's aunt. "I'm sorry about Glinda."

Reva sat on the bed and patted the spot next to her. Thelia studied the pink and silver room. More silver flowers covered pink walls. A cloth covered the top of the bed, forming a canopy. She walked toward Reva and sank down onto one of the softest beds she'd ever been in.

"Glinda and I got along well," Reva said. "Before the curse, it had been a while since we'd seen each other because we lived in different territories. But I should have taken the time. After the curse, I can see why she wanted me dead. I did a lot of terrible things."

When Thelia first came to Oz, Glinda had never mentioned that she was Reva's sister, only that the Wicked Witch needed to be ended.

"Was she your only sibling?" Thelia couldn't help but think about Locasta and the Wicked Witch of the East. When she'd first arrived by tornado, her house had killed the witch of the East.

"Yes, only Glinda. Our parents died when we were very young, so ruling the territories is all we ever knew."

Thelia had started work on a farm very young, but that wasn't anything compared to ruling territories. She glanced around the room. "Where's Ozma?"

"In the kitchen, baking," Reva said. "She was tired of being cooped up. For her entire life it's been like that, hidden as someone else or trapped in that dark place."

Poor Ozma. But then Thelia thought about Reva having to be in that dark place, too. "I'm sorry for what I did." The thought made Thelia want to fold in on herself.

Reva placed a warm hand against Thelia's cold one. "It's not your fault. I don't want you blaming yourself, especially when we have things we need to do."

Thelia met Reva's emerald gaze. "What do you mean?"

"I'm going to ask you for a favor." Reva blew out a breath. "I need you to hold down the forts of the South and the West. You rightfully won them from Langwidere, so they're yours."

Thelia shook her head. "You're back—that means they belong to you."

"No, Thelia, you are powerful, and I think you're the right fae to take charge here." She held up a finger before Thelia could protest. "I had a chat with Ozma and we have a plan. Once I defeat Locasta, because it will happen, I will take control of the North and East, then you and I will share the Emerald City. That only leaves Ozma to reclaim her throne from 'Oz the Bastard.' Then we can all work together to make the Land of Oz a better place again."

"You want me to take care of *this*?" Thelia's voice went up an octave as she pointed out the window. "A ghost town of headless bodies and loose Wheelers?"

"The Wheelers will return to the outskirts near the Deadly Desert. Then you can rebuild the South and West even better than it was before." The edges of Reva's lips lifted, her eyes shifting to the side. "And I think there might be a certain male who wouldn't mind helping you."

Thelia could feel her cheeks grow hot, and she didn't want to talk about Tin with her mother. "Ozma is going with you, then?"

"Only for a little while. She has a journey of her own to make before trying to retrieve the silver slippers from Oz. There's also a special someone waiting for her back home."

"*What?*" Thelia's eyes widened in disbelief. "You can't go alone!"

Reva wrapped her arm around Thelia's shoulders. "Who do you think you inherited your power from?"

That may be so, but Reva had also been overpowered before. "But Locasta..."

A trickle of green lightning pulsed in the center of Reva's palm and Thelia's lips parted at the beauty of it. "After having you, I was drained of magic, and Locasta caught me off guard." Reva's spine straightened and her jaw clenched. "It won't happen this time." The green faded from her hand as if it had never been there.

"Then take Crow with you. He's—"

"Crow can bury himself outside with the heads for all I care," Reva interrupted. "He will *not* be accompanying me."

How did she know Crow was burying heads if she'd been cooped up in the room? Had she been watching Crow from the window?

"Ozma and I will be leaving tomorrow morning," Reva continued.

"I just got you back, though." Thelia knew she could take care of the South and the West, but she couldn't help but fear what Locasta would do. "Let me go with you. I can help now that I have my magic, and you can help me learn how to use it."

"You can't." Reva pulled her close. "If something happened to both of us, then who would take care of this place? Besides, have faith, we will meet again, same as we did yesterday. While we have today, how about you tell me your story, and I'll tell you mine."

Thelia wanted to argue, but she could tell Reva wouldn't change her mind, just as Thelia wouldn't have. "That sounds wonderful," she finally said.

Kansas would always hold a place in Thelia's heart, but Oz was where she was always meant to be, needed to be, wanted to be. She had a lover, a mother, a father, and a home that she would choose to fight for eternally. Now that she was fae, forever was truly possible, and one day, all of Oz would be safe. And that was a promise.

Did you enjoy Tin?

Authors always appreciate reviews, whether long or short.

Want more Faeries of Oz? Check out Crow, Book Two, in the Faeries of Oz series!

Reva spent the last twenty years in her own purgatory, first as the Wicked Witch of the West, then banished to eternity in darkness. Now that she's returned from oblivion, Reva's out for blood. The Northern Witch, Locasta, destroyed Reva's life out of jealousy over Crow. But Reva's love for him is gone, replaced only with the desire for revenge.

Crow wasted years trying to distract his mind after the Wicked Witch—his true love—was vanquished. He'd thought Reva was lost forever until magic brought her back, though their reunion was anything but happy. Reva hates him now as much as she loved him then. He can't blame her—his former lover cursed them both and stole their daughter away. But he's more determined than ever to earn Reva's forgiveness.

When Reva leaves for the North, intent on destroying Locasta, Crow refuses to lose her to the same magic twice. He joins her on the journey, and, as much as Reva loathes him, she knows it's for the best. Traveling is too dangerous on her own, but spending so much time together isn't exactly safe for their hearts either. Hidden away in her castle, the Northern Witch waits to curse Reva and Crow once more. This time they need to put an end to Locasta, or suffer the consequences of the curse forever.

Acknowledgments

Thank you so much to the readers who came on this journey back to Oz with us!

To our families and friends, you are the stars who guide our way. We'd love to give a big shout out to Elle, Tracy, Amber H., Lauren, Lindsay, Loretta, Victoria, and Gerardo for helping us get this story in shape.

Writing Tin and Dorothy's characters were so much fun! And we promise the next book will be just as entertaining!

About the Authors

Candace Robinson spends her days consumed by words and hoping to one day find her own DeLorean time machine. Her life consists of avoiding migraines, admiring Bonsai trees, watching classic movies, and living with her husband and daughter in Texas—where it can be forty degrees one day and eighty the next.

Amber R. Duell was born and raised in a small town in Central New York. While it will always be home, she's constantly moving with her husband and two sons as a military wife. She does her best writing in the middle of the night, surviving the daylight hours with massive amounts of caffeine. When not reading or writing, she enjoys snowboarding, embroidering, and snuggling with her cats.

The Girl in the Clockwork Tower by Lou Wilham

A tale of espionage, lavender hair, and pineapples.

Welcome to Daiwynn where magic is dangerous, but hope is more dangerous still.

For Persinette—a lavender-haired, 24-year-old seer dreaming of adventure and freedom—the steam-powered kingdom of Daiwynn is home. As an Enchanted asset for MOTHER, she aids in Collecting Enchanted and sending them to MOTHER's labor camps.
But when her handler, Gothel, informs Persi that she will be going out into the field for a Collection, she decides it's time to take a stand. Now she must fight her fears and find a way to hide her attempts to aid the Enchanted or risk being sent to the camps herself.

Manu Kelii, Captain of the airship The Defiant Duchess, is 26-years-old and hasn't seen enough excitement—thank you very much. His charismatic smile and flamboyant sense of style earned him a place amongst the Uprising, but his fickle and irresponsible nature has seen to it that their leader doesn't trust him.

Desperate to prove himself, Manu will stop at nothing to aid their mission to overthrow MOTHER and the queen of Daiwynn. So, when the Uprising Leader deposits a small unit of agents on his ship, and tasks him with working side by side with MOTHER asset Persinette to hinder the Collection effort, he finds himself in over his head.

The stakes are high for this unlikely duo. They have only two options; stop MOTHER or thousands more will die—including themselves.

Available
9.23.20

Something in the Shadows By Midnight Tide Publishing

For fans of Moon Called, True Blood, and Vampire Diaries.

You've heard their folktales-saw the carnage they left behind-those creatures, the things lurking deep in the shadows, watching and waiting until the right moment to ensnare its prey.
Four authors dared to tell their stories in this unique collection of wonderfully haunting and frightful thrillers, and even dark romance.
Inside, you'll discover tales of vampires, demons, and humans encountering spirits in these short stories that are sure to keep you up at night!

Available
10.28.20

CPSIA information can be obtained
at www.ICGtesting.com
Printed in the USA
BVHW032353310321
603807BV00001B/55